OWNER

BLOOD BROTHERHOOD

LOKI RENARD

Copyright © 2022 by Loki Renard

Cover by The Bookbrander

All rights reserved.

No part of this book may be reproduced in any form or by any electronic or mechanical means, including information storage and retrieval systems, without written permission from the author, except for the use of brief quotations in a book review.

❀ Created with Vellum

1

Thor

The Blood Brotherhood is a secret cabal of powerful priests and laymen who have dedicated their lives to the eradication of evil on Earth. I was brought into the Brotherhood because of my fearsome powers and my talent for finding anything and anyone, no matter where they might roam. I have slain giants. I have broken the wills of tyrants. I have saved families from the ravages of famine, war, and poverty. I do not mention this out of any sense of ego. I mention it because right now, in my hallowed role as a member of the clandestine Blood Brotherhood, I am staring at a bucket. It is not even a special bucket. It is just a slightly rusty old metal bucket.

To be fair, that is what we are all doing. Myself. Bryn, the somewhat disputed leader of the Blood Brotherhood. Crichton, the demon butler. Mrs Crocombe, the demon cook. And of course, Bryn's wife, Nina, the vessel of angel blood. There is more dark magic and angelic power in this room than in the entirety of the vale. There is great education too, though that is not currently conscious. Steven, keeper of ancient knowledge, snores in an armchair in the corner.

You'd be forgiven for thinking we're engaging in some arcane ritual, but this could not be more mundane.

Plunk

Plunk

Plunk

Water drips into the bucket steadily, in an easy to interpret and predictable rhythm. It's coming from the roof and through the ceiling. It should not be doing either of those things.

The reason for the bucket is complicated and begins over a thousand years ago. Direview Abbey was built in the thirteenth century, and it is showing its age. The roof was replaced around sixty-six years ago. It is time it was replaced again.

"A million pounds," Bryn says. "How can anything possibly cost a million pounds?"

He already knows, because the contractor already told him. These historically listed buildings can't just be fixed with any old materials. They've got to match the original as best as possible. That means craftsmen have to be involved, real craftsmen with degrees in history, not just builders. Then there's the materials. And inflation. And a whole lot of problems none of us can solve by stabbing something, which would be our strong preference.

"The bucket is working," I say. "Could buy a lot of buckets for a million pounds."

"If we're broke," Nina interjects. "Could we sell some of my blood? I hear that fetches a high price?"

Bryn refuses that idea outright. "Only among those who practice dark arts. We are trying to project a legitimate front. One that can produce tax records."

"But you're a priest, and churches are tax exempt."

"That's... that's not how it works. We still have to produce evidence of income, or churches would simply become unquestionable money laundering venues."

"Is that not what they are now?"

"No."

"You're so naive sometimes." She rolls her eyes.

Nina is a lot younger than her husband, and so therefore still imagines she knows everything. It's nice to see her holding onto some of her innocence after all she has been through.

"This place is like a museum. What if we open it to the public?" Bryn makes the suggestion, surprising everybody with what a terrible idea that is for so very many reasons.

"Why don't we open the secret and sacred seat of our Brotherhood to the grubby-fingered public?" Crichton is the first to be overtly offended. He does not like people in general. He finds the general public almost completely intolerable.

"No. I think this is the best idea," Bryn insists, having heard no other ideas whatsoever. "We'll open the gardens and the kitchen to the public in an effort to make some funds to redo the roof. We'll display a few artifacts of interest and sell cotton candy. I can announce it to the congregation, and we can use the internet to attract interest from further afield, so Nina informs me. Thor, are you in?"

"Sure," I say, wanting to be a team player. "Why not."

∽

One Sunday later...

Why not? So many reasons why not, as it turns out. We have erected little stalls in the garden to display our exhibits, which makes me feel like I should have pigtails and a lemonade stand. There is something all too humbling about presenting these parts of ourselves. The visitors have no idea that they are being shown some of the most priceless and arcane objects in existence. Some of them seem to think that this is a fete, and the items are for sale. Other people keep trying to buy raffle tickets. We are a secret brotherhood and this was not a good idea. Bryn is trying far too hard to be normal. I know he wants to do that for Nina, but we have gone too far.

I end up standing at a stall with my most treasured and priceless possession before me, being largely ignored by people who keep asking for more of Mrs Crocombe's hot chips and battered fish.

I think we've all realized that nobody is interested in a museum, but practically everybody is interested in Mrs Crocombe's cooking. This will no doubt be the first and last attempt at a museum-style open house. I can already see impatience written on Bryn's face, and he's fairly patient when it comes to dealing with the public. He is the pastor of this parish. A respected pillar of the community hiding a deep well of darkness and pain. His wife has changed him for the better. Nina is wandering about, a red-headed beauty with an elegance and grace few people naturally enjoy.

She is not for me, but I can admire her beauty and hope that one day...

"Wow, what an incredible artifact." A female voice comes from somewhere near me.

Most of the female people here are either older, younger, or the parent of someone younger. In other words, inextricably entangled in a set of personal circumstances which makes them off-limits for a member of the Brotherhood. I know this is not supposed to be a hookup spot, but I must admit that the English nights have become lonely of late. Living in a big old abbey with two demons, a newlywed couple, and a very old man is not precisely the lifestyle I had in mind when I travelled from the frozen Nordic realms to this green and pleasant land. I suppose I have come today hoping in some small way that someone sees my hammer, as it were, and likes it.

"Hm?"

"The hammer," the young lady says. "That is..." She searches for an adjective. "Amazing!"

I have to look down quite a ways to give her my attention. She's short. 5'2 short. The sort of stature that probably allows her to slip into small places but makes top shelves an astonishing mystery.

She seems to have a real appreciation for ancient Norse craftsmanship. And she's cute. Very cute. Short and curvy with curling dark hair cut at the level of her chin. Her lashes are dark and her eyes are an intense blue. The kind of blue that seems to stare right through me. She's wearing makeup in a way that makes her look as though she's giving the entire world the middle finger. If one doesn't know what that mean, I cannot help one.

I have always had a thing for girls like this. The bad girls, the ones who announce themselves as trouble.

"It's fake, though," she says. "A piece like this would be in a museum if it were real." She smiles as she says it, her brows lifting just a fraction. She wants to see what kind of reaction that statement will get.

"I can assure you it is real. It has been handed down through the generations of my family. And there's no way this will ever end up in a museum. It's still useful."

"Yeah? What do you use it for? Show me."

I take it from the glass case. "It's a functional hammer. See the way the ends are beaten from centuries of labor?"

"Almost looks like there's dried blood on the ends," she says.

I look carefully. Well, damn. There is a little dried blood, and some blonde hair sticking out of a bit of inscription. The DNA of giants reposes on this artifact, which is why I haven't scrubbed it up and polished it until it looks like a cheap replica you might find in any Oslo gift shop.

"You're not from around here, are you?"

"No," I say. "I'm from Norway."

"Very cool. I love the accent. Of course, there's a lot of people indirectly from Norway in the country, considering the whole..." She lowers her voice. "Viking thing."

She is referring to the way my ancestors ravaged their way through this land, spreading their seed among the Anglo-Saxons. That was in 793, so over 1200 years ago. Long enough ago that most people don't consider it taboo, but she speaks about it as if it was a far more recent travesty. For most modern people, the Viking thing is something to make shows about and dress up in. It's like pirates or ninjas; the horror of the past becomes the amusement of the present, a kind of historical bread and circuses.

"May I hold it?"

"It's very heavy."

"Doesn't look that heavy."

"Well, it is."

She smiles at me, as if she knows something she's not supposed to know.

"I can't believe this is here, right here, at Direview. Who would have thought!"

"Indeed."

"What's your name? Let me guess." She has dimples on her cheeks when she smiles. She's adorable. "Thor."

"Yes," I say.

She laughs. "Of course it is."

"Thor Larsen," I say. "At your service."

"What are you doing here, Thor?"

"I am staying with Father Bryn here at the abbey."

"Ah, for long, or?" She lets the question dangle.

"For as long as he has use for me. I am part of the Brotherhood."

"Like a monk?"

"Not in the celibate sense," I say. Then I realize that's not necessarily what she was asking.

She laughs.

"You're funny," she says. "Well, I guess if you're not going to let me hold your hammer, I should see about some fish and chips."

The hammer is humming. Threatening to dance. I have to hope she doesn't notice that. I have to hope that she doesn't notice many of the little oddities around the abbey. We are banking on people bringing their sense of the mundane to this place that is anything but. There are things here no mortal should ever set eyes on. One of them is cooking the popular meals.

I glance down at my hammer again. I'd love to let her taste the power of it, but I know that it's not worth the risk. The insurance alone...

"See you later," she says with one last bright smile. I watch her saunter off toward the line for chips, and that's the last I see of her. Nobody else comes by for about thirty minutes, at which point it doesn't matter anymore because the abbey has caught on fire.

"FIRE!" The scream goes up from what's left of the straggling crowd. I can see smoke near one of the thatched overhangs of an outbuilding. If that goes up, we lose valuable history forever. Over a thousand years gone in a flash. I race toward the smoke, to discover some moron has set a fish and chip wrapper alight and stuffed it in some of the undergrowth that should never have been allowed to grow there. I grab an as yet to burn corner of the wrapper and stamp the flaming mess out on the ground. Chip and fish smear beneath my boot.

"What's this?"

"We let the public in for two minutes and they set the place on fire. They can't help it. It's the residual Norse DNA," Crichton deadpans.

This is no attempt to sack the abbey. This was an attempt to rob me. I run back to my stall, but of course it is already too late. The top of the glass display case has been shattered. There are shards of glass absolutely everywhere. The hammer is gone.

So is the girl.

I raise my voice and begin to stalk the grounds, though I know she's probably already made a run for it. She doesn't look like the type to enjoy cardio, but brains can fix what brawn misses.

"Has anybody seen a short, curvy minx holding a hammer bigger than she is?"

Nobody has seen anything. The remainder of the visitors are politely but firmly shooed out of the abbey.

I curse underneath my breath. To have lost the hammer would be a misfortune, but to have allowed it to be stolen out from under my very nose, that feels like carelessness.

∽

"Yep. There you go," Bryn says, sitting back in his chair and putting his hand to his mouth to hide the smirk. He knows this is a big deal. The biggest deal. But he has been through worse. A missing object is nothing compared to a missing bride.

It's also quite amusing, I suppose, when one watches the video with a level of detachment and sees the way the local wench scammed me from the moment she came up to me. The cameras follow her around to the kitchen, where she has a few handfuls of chips — actually eating them out of her fisted hand like a small scavenging creature — before darting around behind the outhouse, which I now know used to be a quarantine hut for monks who happened to be infected with whatever the latest plague was. She set the wrapper on fire there, then made a big circle out around the bushes before screaming FIRE, panicking everyone, and making me run over like a massive marionette on her strings.

"I like her," Nina says. "She seems cool."

Nina is American, which means she thinks anything reckless is cool. She's also young, approaching her twenty-first birthday fairly soon. The young lady who ripped me off is a little older, perhaps.

"The last thing we need around here is any more bad influences," Bryn says, quirking a brow at his wife.

"I'll find her," I vow. "And I'll get my hammer back."

"Make sure you don't lose anything else in the process," Nina smirks.

"Like what?"

She gives me a sweet smile and tosses her hair, her features assuming an all too knowing expression.

"Like your heart."

2

Anita

I've cut my bloody hand, but that doesn't matter. I have a bit of paper chip wrapper around it and that's enough to stop it dripping blood in an obvious way in the back of the ride share I grabbed with a nice old couple who happened to be leaving around the same time as me.

What a rush! And all totally worth it. I would cut my hand a hundred times over for what's now in my rucksack. We're almost back to town and I'm still out of breath. I'd not run that far or that fast in a long time.

"Would you like some water, dearie?"

The lady offers me a bottle. I take it gratefully and down about half of it. Part of my thirst and dry mouth just comes from sheer adrenaline rather than exertion from exercise.

"Thank you," I say. "That's really nice of you."

We're almost back at the village. I don't know why, but that makes me feel safer.

Direford village sits just above the river Dire, which runs through the valley. The abbey is further up on higher ground, because historically monks and abbeys and nuns and convents were always being ransacked and they needed the extra visibility to hide the good shit away. If I found Thor's fucking hammer sitting out in the open today, I can only imagine what other kinds of relics they have hidden away.

"This is me," I say. "Thanks so much for letting me tag along."

I give the nice old couple a couple of pounds. At least, I try to, but they refuse. They're too nice to take money from someone like me. Someone obviously poor. Someone who has a priceless treasure hidden away.

I hurry through the streets. Obviously, I didn't get out at my actual place. I don't want the oldies to be able to tell the big, muscular Norwegian who just lost one of the most precious relics in existence where I went. I weave through the picturesque, cobbled streets and across the little foot bridges over rivulets that feed the river Dire, and I make my way to the much less romantic part of town where I live.

The rest of the water comes in handy. All this running about and skulking works up a thirst. I just want to get inside as quickly as possible. They'll call the cops for sure, and they'll give them my description and I'm probably going to get a visit from the local plod. Got to take that into consideration.

I go in the front door and scurry up two flights of stairs. I am not pleased to see that the pull-down steps to my attic room are down. Someone's up in my fucking room, and I know just who.

"Get out of my room, Brad!"

Our flat is a shit hole. I'm technically unemployed, and that means I live with six people in a three-bedroom house. Brad was allowed to move in on the condition he slept in the bath at night, but he's always trying to sneak into the bedrooms just to lie on a mattress. It's kind of sad, but I also hate it when he's in my room. That's where I keep my secrets. And my food.

I like being tucked up in the attic. It feels private — or at least, it does when Brad's not invading my personal space. Again, it's not technically a room, not by council regulations. It is a room by my reckoning, though, based on the KEEP OUT sign I've stapled to the trapdoor that sits up in the middle of the hall, right next to the rope that hangs from it so you can pull it down and open it up.

"Sorry!" Brad shoots me an apologetic look as he comes down my steps. "Your cushions are so comfy."

"I am going to staple a cushion to your balls if I ever see you in here again. This is my space. Mine. Get it?"

"Yeah. God. Chill." He cuts his eyes at me and then slouches off like he's the wronged one. Guys always think they're the victims.

I am not going to chill. What I have in my possession is so powerful, so important that I can never leave it behind. My room isn't secure enough. Nowhere is secure enough for what I found today. There's not a temple, not a fortress, not a distant space station manned with hostile beings, nowhere secure enough anywhere in creation. But it doesn't matter. Because this treasure is more than capable of looking after itself.

Clambering up into the attic, I pull the steps up after me. I am immediately shrouded by shadows. It's a dark little space, this attic, but it's my dark little space. There is one window that looks out to the outside world, but I'm keeping the curtains shut for now. Instead, I turn on a little hurricane lamp. It throws a pleasingly diffuse light around the room as I dump my bag down off my back and reach into it.

I wrap my hands around the shaft and I feel a deep sense of power flowing through me.

"Thor's actual hammer," I whisper to myself. The priest might not have known what he had, but I do. I lift it up to inspect it properly for the first time.

It's smaller than I expected it to be. There are some legends that say only Thor can lift his hammer, but obviously that's not true, because I was able to heft it out of the display case and into my rucksack without issue.

I always carry a rucksack. People get used to seeing you with a big bag, and you can put all sorts of things in it without raising suspicion. Except supermarkets and pound stores. They always want you to leave your bag at the door or present it for inspection. I never do either of those things. Misdirection is my game. Most of what I do is what people on the internet call social engineering. People off the internet call it social engineering too, but not as often.

I can't stop looking at this hammer. It is both powerful and exquisite. Legend has it that the god Thor murdered a bunch of giants after they stole it and tried to ransom it.

Mjollnir is its true name. Now technically, it's not actually an item of legend. But it is obviously a very ancient attempt to embody that legend.

The runes hammered into the metal must have been placed there by a hand many thousands of years ago. Whenever I get to touch anything this old, I feel energies coursing through it. People must have been incredibly powerful back then. I wonder what made us so weak in modern times. We have so much more now. We have powers the ancients would have considered to be the highest magic, but I don't get this sense when I touch an iPhone.

Maybe, in the distant future, someone will unbox a smart phone and experience this feeling of reverence imagining the world as it exists now. Maybe they'll imagine someone like me, and maybe they'll imagine that I was someone who mattered.

Anyway. I am hungry. I need to find something to eat. There's pot noodle in the cupboard next to me. I have my own kettle and I keep it primed. I keep a stash of nonperishable foods in my room. The idea is I don't have to go out if I don't want to. I quite often don't want to.

Brad was stealing from my food stash. I don't keep anything shiny out and about. I keep the place looking, well, poor. I got the mattress I sleep on from a second-hand store. It is lumpy and uncomfortable. I'm thinking about swapping it out for a hammock if I can find one to steal.

Everything I have, I have scavenged, borrowed, or outright stolen. I do not work. It's a matter of principle. Work is a trap, in my view. You get a job, you get tied into the system. I'm stuck inside the system too, but I'm not beholden to it.

At least, that's what I tell myself. I'm not a loser if I choose to lose, right?

A lot of people would try to sell this hammer. But I already know there's no way to sell it and get its true value. It won't be appreciated for all it is worth by anyone — anyone except its true owner. Thor.

I will eventually sell it back to him. But not yet. I'll wait until he's desperate. I'll wait until he'll pay anything to get it back — and that's when I'll get everything.

Thor

"We should call the police," Steven says. He's furious to discover that my hammer has been taken.

"I am not calling the police. The last thing we need are more normal people involved in this situation. The mundane has infected our abbey and desecrated an artifact of irreplaceable value. We wouldn't even be able to explain what it was she took without sounding completely bonkers," Bryn says.

Steven makes a set of generally offended sounds. "You know, she tried to burn the bloody place down in order to get it. She's an arsonist. That's worse than a thief. She's damn well dangerous. She could be back for more. We could find her creeping in the windows late at night, going through our drawers and smalls…"

The mention of Steven's smalls draws a few raised brows, but we know what he means. We made three hundred and twenty pounds in fish and chip sales and we've lost something irreplaceable.

It's time I inserted my own opinion into this mess.

"I'll find her. She's a local. I know that much. And Direford is not that large a village. Someone will inevitably know her. I just need to make some inquiries. I found Nina in London in a matter of days. How hard could it be?"

"Famous last words," Steven says. "I thought it would come when you called?"

"It's a hammer, not a dog," I remind him.

"Sure, but it's a magical hammer."

"It is a relic. It is an object of great worth and even greater significance. We cannot afford to lose this. Better the entire abbey burn down than this relic remain in the hands of the mundane."

"Well," Bryn says. "Let's not go mad about it."

It's too late. I am already mad. I know my quarry very well. She's short. She's naughty. She's in need of a rough and thorough dose of discipline. When I catch her, I will make her more sore than she's even been in her short and sorry life.

3

Anita

Direford is a little village. Part of it is picturesque and old. The other part of it is new and industrial. This place is industrial adjacent. Constructed right around the time everybody decided that making buildings look appealing was a waste of fucking time and instead put all their effort into making them as bland and square and depressing as possible. At least this place has an attic. I like being up high, being able to look down on others, see them coming for me. I'm like a cat that way.

I peek out the window, parting the black shade cloth I have been using for curtains. There's nothing on the street. Nothing bar the usual, anyway. A couple of homeless people that the council insists aren't actually homeless. Like they're just experimental artists working on various ways to shelter under tarps.

Anyway, they're there. Nobody else is. It's a quiet time of day. Later on, there will be some stragglers coming back from work. Sometimes I hang about on the street and see if they drop something. I don't think I will today. Today I just want to look at this treasure, enjoy it for as long as I can.

THUDDDDABANG!

A clap of thunder heralds the day turning dark. I guess a storm is rolling in. Little weird for this time of year, but the weather has been weird for a while now. Everybody has noticed it. It's a whole thing.

The tin roofing that's been used to patch what should be tiles over my head starts to rattle with hail. If you were paranoid, you might think it was the attempt of some massive entity to get in. Maybe to get the hammer back. If I'm not mistaken, the hammer is kind of vibrating with the weather. Probably some kind of old resonance in the hollow shaft.

Stealing expensive and important things is a workout for the nervous system. Can't give into panic. Can't let my conscience, whatever's left of it, get the better of me. If I do that, then I've really got nothing to trade on at all.

∽

Stephanie nabs me as I'm going down the stairs. She's too good for this flat, and too good for this town. She was made for bigger, better things. But her boyfriend, Tom, is a bricklayer here and he doesn't want to move to London, so here she is, waiting for him to put a ring on it. It's not going to happen, but I'm not going to be the messenger who takes that bullet.

"Have you got your portion of the rent?"

"No. But I will soon. I'll have enough for all of us."

"You're always saying things like that. I need the rent by tomorrow, or you need to move out."

"How much do you need?"

"Sixty pounds."

"I'll get it. Don't worry."

"Sixty pounds is for this week. Six hundred and sixty pounds for the last eleven weeks you haven't paid."

I feign surprise. "Wow, has it been that long?"

"It has. I should evict you."

Her threat is somewhat hollow. See, I'm not really technically even a tenant, and yet I am living here, so by the way the laws are set up, I'm kind of entitled to stay. Sort of. Anyway, the one thing I am sure about is that Stephanie would be in all kinds of trouble for subletting to me. This place is way over occupancy.

Like I said, Stephanie was made for bigger, better things. She was made to fuck poor people over in London or maybe Manchester. Or hell, internationally. Berlin. Manila. New York. There's no end of places she could screw her fellow human out of a dollar. But we're lucky to have her here because she always finds the best deals. And that's why I live in an uninsulated attic as the resident fire risk. Because it's a good deal.

I was going to let the big guy sweat it out for a week or two, but I guess I have a call to make now. Their number is online. They're easy to find. Unlike me.

"Hello? Is that Direview Abbey? Yes. Hi. I'd like to speak to Thor, please."

There's a soft-spoken man on the other end of the line who says that he will get Thor for me. He seems nice. I don't remember him from the open house, but then again, I'm not entirely certain I remember anybody besides...

"Thor."

I feel a great thrill at hearing his voice. It's deep and gravelly, and accented.

"Hi, Thor. You might remember me from earlier?"

"Girl," he growls. Fuck. I could come right now. "Bring me back my hammer."

"I'd love to. I'd really love to. I just need a hundred thousand pounds."

"You stole my hammer, and now you wish to ransom it back to me? Girl, you do not know who you are crossing, and you know even less what you have in your possession. Bring it back to me at once, and I will spare you the worst of the consequences. If you make me find you, I will thrash you to within an inch of your life. I will make you feel pain unlike any you've ever felt. I..."

I'm not going to lie. His threats are turning me on. He's just so intense and angry. And hot. I can imagine the way his eyes must be glinting like two steel bolts about to strike home. I bet his muscles are bulging and flexing right now with the urge to get his hands on me.

"Yeah? What kind of pain? Be specific."

"I am going to cane you, girl. A stroke for every hour you keep my hammer away from me."

"Wow. A punishment they used to use on schoolgirls. Terrifying."

"You want it to be worse?"

I laugh. He is never going to put hands on me. He has no idea where I am. If he did, he'd be here already.

"I want you to pay me and stop making weak little girl threats."

He snarls down the line. "There is no threat that will convince you to do the sensible thing, because you are yet to know true pain and suffering. I will change both those things."

"Pay me. My money."

"It's not your money, and the fact that you think I have a hundred thousand pounds to give to the local rip-off artist is testament to how foolish you are."

"Alright. Fifty thousand."

He laughs. His mirth is cold like rolling thunder.

"You are so far out of your depth, little girl. Bring the hammer back to the abbey and we will be done."

"I want money. Make me an offer."

"You will not get a penny from me, girl."

"Then you won't get your hammer back. Bye."

I disconnect the call. I didn't expect him to agree to give me a hundred thousand pounds right away, but I bet he can scrape together at least ten thousand. Am I kind of a twat for demanding money from a church group trying to raise funds for a new roof? Yeah. Definitely. But their problem isn't my problem. I am their problem.

Unfortunately, this means that I'm not going to be getting the rent money today. Sixty pounds might as well be a hundred thousand pounds with the amount of money I have. Oh well. There's always tomorrow.

4

Tomorrow comes at me hard.

It comes with someone pulling down the stairs to my room and coming up them. Stephanie. She sticks her head through the hole in my floor and glares at me with her unhappy face.

"I need that money, or you can move your things out today. I mean it, Anita. We're covering your share of the rent and it's not fair. You need to get a job."

"I have a job," I tell her. "I'm going to get paid very soon, I promise."

She frowns at me. Meanwhile, I find it hard to keep a straight face because when people stick their heads up the hole the way she has done, they basically look like disembodied heads. "You've promised far too many times for me to believe you."

"Alright, well, if you want me to leave, I assume you've got the eviction papers."

"Don't be a dickhead," she says. "Just get the money. Or something like the money."

She dips out, leaving me to my increasingly desperate circumstances. I really didn't want to call him back this soon. The timeline isn't good. We're talking so much right now it feels like we're practically dating. Hell, there are men I've been with who talked to me less than Thor.

Thor answers the phone with his name. I don't know who actually does that.

"Thor."

"Hi. What about, say, a thousand pounds?"

"Not a pound. Not a penny."

"What about a hundred pounds?"

He's got to say yes to that. A hundred pounds is nothing. I feel stupid even asking for that.

The dial tone is my only response.

"Fucking hell," I curse. "Wanker!"

I dial again. I can't believe he hung up on me. I suppose it is his right, but it does seem rude. I get to steal things and bribe people, but hanging up on others, well. How very dare he.

"Girl." An impatient voice answers. I don't know this one. Or maybe I do. It's an English accent, a refined one. Not the soft-spoken servile voice who first got me Thor. This is someone who fancies himself in charge.

"Who is this? I want to talk to Thor."

"Thor's not going to talk to you. And you're not getting any money. From any of us. Return the hammer before it gets you into real trouble. There's worse things to be than broke. Trust me."

"Who are you?"

"I am Father Bryn. Direview Abbey is my ancestral home, and Thor is my brother. In crossing him, you have crossed me. What is your name?"

"Obviously, I'm not going to tell you that. And obviously the hammer means something to you all. So why don't you cough up some money. I'm barely asking for anything. Just a sweet ten thousand pounds."

"It was a hundred last call."

"That was last call. Then he hung up on me and that made me angry. It's back to ten thousand. That's a ninety-percent discount on the original hundred thousand. I'm practically giving this thing away here!"

There's a pause. I think he might be laughing. Yeah. There it is. The inhale followed by those short little exhales. He's laughing. This is definitely time to cut the call. On a high note. Well, sort of. I'm still bloody broke.

Thor

Bryn hangs up the phone. He is smirking, and not because he wants to. I heard the conversation. The girl is relentless. "We are in real trouble here. And she is in..." He lets out a long exhale. "We've got to catch her."

"How do we do that? I can't sense the hammer right now, and we can't call the police. Best I can think of is to wait until I feel the hammer again. And by the time that happens..."

"Talk to her next time she calls. Not about the hammer. Or, hell. Tell her we're going to give her the money. We'll trap her."

"I think she's smart enough to evade a trap."

"Maybe. Maybe not. She's greedy. Greedy trumps smart at least fifty percent of the time."

Ring Ring! The phone is going again.

"Right on cue," Bryn says. He's pleased to have predicted her impatience. I'm not so thrilled.

I answer. No pleasantries. "We'll give you a thousand pounds," I say. "That's all we have to spare, and it's more than you deserve. Bring the hammer to the front of the abbey at midnight."

"Absolutely not. We'll do it in Direford. In the park. By the war memorial. At three pm today."

She's a cocky little thing. She doesn't skip a beat while trying to brazenly rip me off. She seems unable to feel shame, and that's concerning for a whole host of reasons.

"I don't think so."

"Why? Because you can't rip me off in the park in front of everybody?"

"Because two priests handing over a thousand pounds is going to draw attention."

"I'm not asking you to stick it in my g-string. Put it in an envelope. I'll bring the hammer in a bag. We do the switch on the park bench. Easy. Nobody gets hurt."

"How do we know you're giving us the real hammer? How do you know we're giving you real cash? We need to be somewhere we can each inspect the goods. At the abbey. Tonight."

"I don't think so."

"Do you want the money or not?"

"I don't know. Do I want the money? What is money? And is a thousand pounds enough, really? All this risk you're asking me to take, the obvious chance of a double cross. Let me think about it. I'll call you back. You'll still be on this number? 'Course you will be."

The line goes dead again. She's gone. Out of my influence. With my bloody hammer. I am torn between cold rage enough to destroy the entire village of Direview or admiring her nerve.

"She," Bryn points at the phone, "is fucking with us."

"Why? She wants her money."

"Or she wants something even harder to come by these days," he suggests.

"What's that?"

"Trouble."

"Oh, she's found plenty of that. I vow that."

5

Thor

We are waiting by the abbey gates in the moonlight. It is late, almost midnight, and a summer breeze plays across the valley. It would almost be romantic if Bryn weren't here, and if I wasn't about to steal my recalcitrant hammer back from the wretch who dared cross me.

"She's not coming, is she?"

"She'll be here." Bryn is so confident, as if he knows something I don't. That is just the way he speaks, however. It's one of his many qualities that make him suited to leadership. No matter how bad things get, Bryn always sounds like he knows what's going on. And has wisdom to impart.

"Remember, no matter how much you want to beat her, you cannot lay a finger on her. She's not one of us. She's a civilian, as it were. And we don't know who she is, or who she is connected to. Which means if you assault her, you're inviting legal scrutiny of the kind we literally cannot afford."

"So when you whip your wife..."

"I don't whip my wife."

"You know what I mean. You punished her several times before you were married."

"That was different for a whole host of reasons. This is a local stranger. We cannot antagonize the locals. We exist here in plain sight. We have to maintain a veneer of respectability. So curb your impulses, Thor. After tonight, she will be banished from the grounds. You will not see her again. Ever."

Something in me instinctively rebels against that sentiment, but I do not argue. Bryn may speak like he is the boss, but in truth we are equals and he has no right to tell me what I can and cannot do.

"Hello, boys!"

She's come, clad in darkness like the night. It's just a hoodie and black jeans, but she'd make anything look mysterious. There is something of the witch about this young woman, both in attitude and temperament.

She's keeping her distance, her eyes wary but also dancing with mischief. I knew she was trouble the moment I saw her. I find myself glad to see her a second time, pleased to lay eyes on her simply because she is pretty. I am also furious to see her because she is an absolute wretch.

There's a case in her hand. A small tool box.

"What better place to store a hammer?" She smirks and lifts it up for me to see better. That flimsy plastic is all that stands between me and my relic. Unbelievable. She has taken the sacred and made it mundane. I hope, for a mad moment, that she has not damaged it. Then I remember that the hammer is not easy to harm. She is much softer than it, in every way.

"Let's make this exchange," Bryn says. "Put the hammer down and back away. We will put the envelope down and back away. Then we can both take what we came for. Fair?"

I wish he wasn't here. I know he thinks he is helping, but this is beginning to feel a lot more like interference. I can handle one bad little girl by myself.

I watch her put the case down. Ten or so meters away, Bryn puts the envelope down. We both make a dash for our respective packages, and we are both swiftly disappointed.

"This a hammer from a hardware store," I growl.

She tosses the contents of the envelope on the ground. "And this is Monopoly money. You priests are liars, aren't you. Aren't there rules against that?"

"As I suspected," Bryn chuckles. "We both came to cheat one another. No harm, no foul."

He's wrong. Plenty of harm and a lot of foul. I am done with diplomacy. I want my fucking hammer. And I want my bloody revenge. I grab the girl, picking her up off the ground with my hands fisted in her hoodie. I am going to hurt her. I am going to hear her scream. I want to see the terror in her eyes. I want to hear her beg for the mercy she absolutely does not deserve.

"Let me go," she hisses against my nose. "Or you'll never see your poxy trinket again."

I don't want to let her go. I want to rip these clothes off her and I want to whip her curvaceous little rear with anything and everything I can get my hands on.

"Thor..." Bryn reaches out and touches my shoulder. "Put her down."

"Listen to your boss," she says.

"He's not my boss. He's my brother. I don't answer to him. But after tonight, you're absolutely going to answer to me."

I might not have my hammer, but I will have her respect.

I carry her over to the bench near the inner wall and I throw her over my lap. She kicks and struggles, but her much shorter feminine frame is no match for my strength. I know Bryn doesn't approve of what I'm doing. He'd say she's not mine. I have no authority. I don't care. She needs a good thrashing a lot more than she needs a thousand pounds.

"Let me go, you lying psycho!"

She's screaming at the top of her lungs. But there's nobody to hear her. Nobody besides us. She didn't want to come because something like this might happen, and now it is happening.

Her jeans come down with one decent tug to the waistband. Her rear is full and generously shaped. Made to be thrashed, I think, but sadly bereft of all the punishments it should have received over the years.

She knows what is coming, because it is no more and no less than what I have promised her.

"Don't! Don't you fucking dare! If you touch me, then... OW!"

She squeals in such a satisfying way when my palm meets her cheeks. My big hand has an impressive span. I can't reach across both at the same time, and that's fine. I'll spank her twice as long and twice as hard.

"I'm never going to give you the hammer now you're doing this!"

"Yes. You are. I am going to make you so sore and so sorry you beg to bring my hammer back."

"Get fucked, mate!"

Of course she's refusing at this point. I've only just started. Spanking her is the most satisfying thing I have done in a very long time. I think I will spank her from now until sunrise, and maybe all the way through to lunch time. The way she feels over my lap is perfect. She has a nice weight and lovely curves. She may be a thief, a liar, and an arsonist, but she is quite physically pleasing.

Bryn is looking on with a dour expression, mostly aimed at me. I don't care if he approves or not. I'm doing this.

I start to spank her properly, just as I promised I would.

Her skin is perfect under my hand, soft and warm and yielding to each of the punishing slaps I land. I am entirely focused on one task now, making her sorry.

Anita

This really fucking hurts. My ass is absolutely burning and swollen and like he promised, sore. There's no way I'm giving his fucking hammer back now.

He's spanked me at least a dozen times. Every time his hand lands it feels more like leather being dashed across my ass with a great and powerful weight behind it. The pain isn't the worst part, though. It's being held like this. Treated like this. I'm not fond of consequences at the best of times, and this is so fucking humiliating I can hardly stand it.

He pauses for a blessed moment to ask a stupid fucking question.

"What do you have to say for yourself?"

"The price is a hundred thousand pounds. No. A million pounds. No. Ten million pounds! Ten fucking million pounds, that's what it is going to take for you to get a piece of the hammer back. One little piece. Because that's what I'm going to fucking do, mate. I'm going to run that fucking thing through a bandsaw, and then I'm going to melt the head down, and..."

"I guess we're not done," he growls.

He doesn't know who he is trying to hurt. I've had the shit kicked out of me more times than I can count. He starts spanking me again. My screams of outrage are starting to become screams of aching pain. He's too fucking big to resist. He's a huge, vengeful monster, and I don't know that I'm going to survive this.

"Enough. ENOUGH!" Bryn intervenes. "She's not giving in. And she's not going to. Punishment doesn't work because it hurts. It works because the person receiving it wants the approval and the forgiveness of the punisher. She doesn't know you, doesn't like you, and doesn't care about you. You can beat her into submission, but I don't think you want to do that. That gets nasty. And messy. And usually bloody."

"Everything he said," I agree. "Especially the part about not liking you."

Thor's got to listen to me now.

"Get me a switch," he says to Bryn.

"I'm not getting you anything, except perhaps a lawyer," Bryn sighs.

Thor growls and picks me up again. He hauls me about without effort, showing me just how fucked I am. I can never risk letting him get his massive hands on me again, that much is for absolute certain.

"Make him let me go!" I appeal to Bryn. "I'm going to have this whole fucking place shut down, I am. I'm going to make you all regret the day you met me."

Thor reaches a birch tree, pulls off a thin, whippy branch and starts in on me with that, lifting his foot up on a rock and holding me over his muscular thigh. This guy is an absolute unit, so much larger than me, monstrously cruel.

Yes, tormenting him was probably a bad idea. A very bad idea. Should have sent him a note. That would have riled him up less. It was fun while it lasted. Like most things that are fun while they last, it's not at all fun now.

I soon learn that the switch is a different kind of torment. "Ow! Ow! Fucking! Ow!" Every time it lands, I curse and gasp. He's painting my tender, swollen cheeks with thin lines of pure pain. He's taken my dignity. He's made me feel like an urchin in the grip of a furious lord.

"You're lucky this is all that is happening to you," Thor growls. "You deserve to be thrashed every day of your disobedient life until you learn basic respect for others and their property, you insolent little thief."

I am feeling that heat again. The heat I'm not supposed to be feeling. It's more like arousal, and it's coming from the inferno in my ass, and the feeling I get low in my belly when he lectures me. It's fucking hot.

"Unless you intend on making her bleed, it's time to let her go." Bryn attempts to intercede again, but this time instead of feeling appreciative of his interference, I just want him to fuck off. This is between me and the big blond bloke.

"I don't want to let her go," Thor says. I feel him snug me a little closer, reflexively. I melt, hearing him say that. Of course I want to escape my punishment, but it is nice being held. God, I am pathetic, aren't I.

"You can't carry her around forever," Bryn says practically. "And the second you let her go, she's going to run. Straight to the nearest police station, I imagine."

"I'm not a snitch. I'm just going to keep your fucking hammer. I'll send you little slivers…. OW!"

I scream as that infernal branch makes fresh, harsh contact with my ass.

Suddenly, Father Bryn's dark eyes are before mine. He has crouched down to be on my punished level.

"I have tried to save you, but you appear to be insistent on not being saved. Not a word of contrition, not a sympathetic apology, nothing but impudence." His eyes flick up to Thor above me. "There is one reason you should let her go," he says. "She's a masochist."

"I am not!"

I lose the warmth and strength of Thor's big arm as he releases me. I am forced to scramble to pull my jeans back up over my aching arse. Fuck. I can't believe Bryn managed to talk me out of that, and right before I really started to enjoy it.

"I think you're right," he says, looking at me judgmentally. Like I'm the freak. Like I'm not a priest who lures young women to his abbey late at night. Like I've done something wrong.

"Well, get fucked," I say. This is my one chance to run, and hotness aside, I'm going to take it. I dash away, the harsh fabric of my jeans rubbing against the welts on my arse, because of course my underwear didn't manage to come all the way up while I was yanking it around and has instead bunched under my cheeks in a useless roll.

Either one of them could probably catch me in the first thirty seconds or so of running, but they're too busy being smug and priestly and thinking they've come to some great revelation to realize that letting me go still means letting the hammer go too, duh.

I scurry into the night, through the bushes, and am to all intents and purposes, gone.

6

Anita

I wake up the next morning sore and hungry. It's not a great combination. My second-hand mattress has never felt so uncomfortable before.

Stephanie hasn't bothered me with her eviction threats today, but I'm sure she'll stop by later to put me out on the street.

The supermarket is my favorite place to go shopping. And by shopping, I of course mean shoplifting, or more lately, scrounging. I've got a guy on the inside who hooks me up with stuff that would otherwise be thrown out. He's cool and he's kind of the reason I eat.

But I don't see him when I first go in. Usually I know if he's got something for me because he stacks the avocados sideways. The more avocados stacked sideways, the better the haul will be.

Today, all the avocados are stacked perfectly upright. Weird. It's Tuesday, and that's his day on. Craig never misses work. Ever. The guy is like old clockwork.

I go up to one of his friends. Wendy also always on Tuesdays. Wendy turns a blind eye more than most. She's cool, but not as cool as Craig.

"Where's Craig?"

"We don't know. Never showed up for work since about a month ago."

"How could it have been a month since I was here?"

She shrugs. I guess time has gotten away on me. Paying bills and getting food have kind of become oddly unimportant lately. I've been getting by on just whatever. Sometimes I forget to eat. I'm maintaining mass though, so I must be doing something right, or something quite wrong.

I leave the supermarket, though not without stealing a sweetie from the racks where they put sweeties to try to make you impulse buy them. It works on me too, just without the buying part.

Guess I've got an old guy to call on.

Craig lives in an old flat in the better part of the village. I think he bought it years ago, before he worked in the supermarket. When prices were a lot lower, and he had a lot more money. I've never had what you might call a full and proper conversation with Craig, but I always knew something had gone really bloody wrong in his life somewhere along the way.

Anyway, it's nice old stone cottage with ivy clambering up the walls and a thatched roof. It's the sort of place people dream of having to call their own when they're not thinking about the upkeep of living in a biodegradable cottage. Though I guess, strictly speaking, everything is biodegradable if you wait long enough.

I knock on the door. There's no response, so I let myself in. There's a key up on the ledge above the door around the back. He told me that once. Stephanie thinks he was hitting on me, but I think it was worse. I think he was really fucking lonely.

MAROW!

His cat is indoors, poor thing! The cat is not happy. Craig calls him Craig Junior. Craig Junior is a big un-neutered ginger tom with a face like a pancake and a yowl like an orgasmic banshee.

I feed the cat, because, well, only a psychopath wouldn't feed the cat. I'm now worried about Craig. Seems like nobody has even noticed he's missing. Fuck. What if he's not missing? What if he's lying in one of these rooms? It doesn't smell like someone has become dearly departed in here, but maybe the conditions are correct for a kind of mummification. I've heard that's possible. Things just need to be the right kind of dry and you get perfectly preserved…

I push open the toilet door. That's where irony says he'll be. He's not there. There's nothing in there but three scraps of paper clinging to the loo roll.

I always thought that Craig's place would be full of cool shit. But it's really not. It's full of disposables. Stuff that's meant to be thrown away. Postcards taken from racks of destinations he never visited and stuck into mirror frames in a sad little attempt at decoration. This is the flat of a man who never knew what happiness should look like but tried to approximate it anyway.

There's an old phone on the table. I pick it up and dial for help.

"Hello? Police? I'd like to report a missing person. His name's Craig. What's his last name? I don't know. I just know him from work. He hasn't been in for like a week. No, I don't work with him. I know him from his work. He's not there. What? Yes, I've heard of a holiday."

Suffice to say, they're not taking me seriously. The woman on the other end of the line sounds like she couldn't give less of a shit. Maybe even like she'd be happy if Craig was gone forever. There's a total lack of sympathy in her tone, a sort of burned-out weariness.

"I'm sorry, what was your name? PC Pendragon, is it? Right. Well. I'm going to make a note of having reported this now, so if he shows up in the river or god knows where else, then I can point out that you've not bothered to follow up even a little bit. Alright, thanks so much, bye for now. Bye then!" I hang up. I like these old phones. Very satisfying to slam the receiver down.

I check Craig's cupboards for food. Alright. Some noodles. Always good. I stuff them into my rucksack, taking as much as I can. There's a couple of cans of baked beans. Got to get those. And a can of chicken soup. I take that just so I can enjoy the way it slides out all thick and congealed later.

THUNK

The front door opens. Shit. I'm going to have to explain to Craig what I'm doing in his house, and why I reported him missing. I've just become a version of Brad I never wanted to be.

I'm just about to call out, when I realize that whoever is coming through the door isn't Craig. It is way larger. Way taller. Something in my gut tells me to hide.

I flatten myself against the kitchen cabinets, and from there I shuffle inside the pantry.

"Wo ist das shiesse?"

He's speaking German. This means he's not from around here.

Interesting, though, that I've run into the descendants of a second set of historically invasive barbarians in one day. The Germanic tribes don't get as much credit as the Vikings, but that's basically a marketing issue.

"Ich habe keine Ahnung," someone else replies. It's a female voice. She sounds annoyed and somewhat bored. She also sounds like she's on speakerphone. So the man is here alone, but with an accomplice elsewhere.

He starts tearing the house up. And I do mean literally tearing the house up. I can hear furniture being broken, doors being ripped off cabinets, drawers pulled out, all the contents thrown to the ground and rifled through. He's snorting and snarling like an animal, scaring the shit out of me. He's also getting closer.

I've not been this scared in a long time. Definitely not when the priests had me. As angry as they were, they didn't have this kind of energy. This is a rage that will tear people apart as easily as kitchen cabinetry.

I plunge my hand into my rucksack. I have the hammer. That's all I have to defend myself — and I do intend to defend myself.

He rips open the pantry door and I act almost before I've had a chance to think about it. He's a big, ugly bastard, his features twisted with the kind of fury that makes a man look more like an animal.

My hands are lifted high above my head. That's not the motion my instincts want me to make. They want me to curl up in a ball and beg for my life. But my arms are being pulled up. It's almost like the hammer is acting on its own, using me as the tool rather than the other way around.

He looks at me. I look at him. He lets out a growl, reaches for me, and that is the last thing he ever does.

I bring the hammer down. Hard. Harder than I knew I was capable of hitting anybody. I feel the hammer hit his skull and I feel his skull break like an eggshell cracking on the corner of a kitchen counter.

There is a clap of thunder and the massive man collapses. There's blood fucking everywhere. Instantly. A pool of it spreading all over the messy floor, coming right up to my toes. I'm going to have to go through his blood to get out of here.

At the same time as the man dies, lightning claps. Outside the leadlight kitchen window I can see that the day has gone dark. Rain is suddenly pouring, and the wind is howling. It was sunny not half an hour ago. But I can't worry too much about the weather, because I am trying very hard to make the mental adjustment to having just fucking killed someone. I've done a lot of terrible things in my life, but I have never killed anybody before.

I don't even know who he was. Might have been a lost German tourist for all I know. My god. What if I've killed a German tourist? I mean, a man. That's all that matters. Someone's brains have just been bashed out and it's my fault. Because I physically did it. With a mythical hammer. That works pretty much the same way a modern hammer does. Probably. I don't know. I've never hit anyone in the fucking head with a hammer before. Am I freaking out? I am definitely freaking out.

Now there's only one thing left to do.

Run.

T*hor*

I am in Direford, making some inquiries. It's not that big a village. Someone is going to know who the curvy little Gothic chick is. I have a still from the security footage and I'm asking about the sorts of places she might work or go. The record store. A cafe. I have a suspicion that a couple of people I've spoken to do know who she is, but nobody has said anything of use.

"Never seen her," a tattooed young man tells me.

The way that his pierced brows rose when I showed him the picture makes me think that's very untrue.

"Never seen her?"

"No. Definitely not. Who are you?"

"Father Larsen."

"Uh huh. Why is a priest looking for ... her?"

"I have something for her. A small inheritance." I hand him a twenty pound note. Enough to perk his interest and greed. "Let me know if you do see her. There's more."

"Well, actually. Now you mention it..."

Before he can tell me a new lie, the sky opens and my silent hammer calls me with a voice of thunder. I dash outdoors, ignoring the all-too-late information being spouted behind me. I know where she is. I know where my hammer is. And I know that it has been used.

My hammer should not respond to the will of any other than myself. It should certainly not open up the heavens for a mere human. What is happening? Why is this little English village the site of so much strangeness?

Having seen where the lightning struck, I know where to go. It is not far from where I am. Just a few streets over. I break into a run, feeling the residual static electricity left in the air sparking against my skin. I feel like a hound giving chase to his prey, a beast with a singular intention to reclaim what is his. I do not have to go far to find it.

The girl is running as fast as she can away from the scene of what I can assume is a crime scene. I overhaul her easily in a few steps and grab her around the waist. I'm not letting go of her again. Not for anything. I am not letting her out of my sight.

My car is not far away. Fortunately, the thunder and rain has sent the general public scuttling for cover and nobody sees me bundle the girl into my car like a sack of proverbial potatoes.

She's crying hysterically as we pull away back to the abbey, making incoherent pleas for mercy. I turn my head over my shoulder for one brief moment and make harsh eye contact with her.

"Do you have the hammer?"

"Yes," she sobs. "In my rucksack."

"Good. Put your seatbelt on."

I don't have any patience for tears. Not from her. She'll get no mercy from me.

Anita

What have I done? I always knew that one day I'd go too far. I just didn't know how far I was going to go. Not that I didn't think someone would end up dead. I just thought it would be, I don't know. Me?

Stealing stuff is bad. Not just, I now suddenly realize, because people don't like it when you steal things, but because of what it leads you to next. One minute you're swiping a cool hammer, the next you've killed someone with that cool hammer. Like most life lessons, it comes just too late to be useful. I sit next to Thor with my eyes full of tears, and my fingers wrapped around the shaft of the *murder weapon*.

Fuck. Why am I holding this? I don't even remember getting it out of my bag. I'm drawn to this tool, even after what I just did with it.

"You can give that back," Thor says, suddenly noticing that I still have it. He grasps it just underneath the head, fisting the shaft. Putting his fingerprints all the fuck over the *murder weapon.*

As soon as he takes the hammer, the rain stops. I barely notice that, because those two words keep italicizing themselves in my head. *Murder weapon*, as wielded by a *murderer*. Me. I put my face in my hands and cry because I don't want to be a murderer. I want to be what I was before. Innocent. Okay, not innocent, but a petty criminal. What I've just done will bump me up all the security levels when I inevitably end up in prison.

That thought makes me sob even harder. Thor's not saying anything. He's just grimly driving me toward whatever Fate has in store for me next. His presence is electric and heavy but comforting in a weird way. I know he's not going to let me do anything else terrible. While I'm in his presence I'm safe from the new scariest thing in my life: myself.

Before I know it, we're back at Direview Abbey, winding up the hill into the sunset. The abbey seems very imposing with the sun going down behind it. Ominous and turreted and generally filled with secrets that are probably quite terrible, now I think about it. I suppose I fit there, given that I am also quite terrible.

"It was like a fuckin' toy egg," I whisper to myself.

Thor glances over at me.

"Don't keep playing the incident over in your head," he says. "It won't help."

We draw up to the back of the abbey. I didn't check out back here when I was casing the joint last time. I was going to, but I saw the hammer and the rest is obviously history now. The back of the place is just as impressive as the front, but in a different way. It is gothic and foreboding, cast in shadows.

There's a barred gate in a lower hollow of the house, sort of like a basement entrance. I imagine at one time this is where deliveries came for the monks. Now this is where Thor grabs me and drags me down moss-covered stone stairs, into the depths of the abbey.

I don't know what I was expecting to find. A dusty old wine cellar, maybe. It's not that. It's not that at all.

"This is a dungeon," I exclaim. That's literally what it is. There are cells down here in the little sectioned off area I find myself in. Like jail cells, they're all bars and no walls. No privacy, save for a sort of semi circle of stone around the commode.

"Yes. It's where I intend to deal with you."

He opens the nearest cell and nudges me inside, closing the doors behind me, but not without snatching my rucksack from me first. He's leaving me here in my filthy, bloody clothes. This isn't legal. But what right do I have to complain?

I don't want to be left here. I don't want to be alone with my thoughts.

"You can't leave me here. I'm covered in bits of brain. I need a shower."

"There's a shower above the toilet," he indicates a head suspended from the ceiling. I didn't notice that because there's too many weird things to notice here.

"Why do priests have a place to keep people imprisoned? What's wrong with you all?"

"You just asked for a shower to get the brain off you," he reminds me. "This is not the time to ask what's wrong with me. Get your clothes off. I'll turn the water on for five minutes. There's soap on the ledge there."

He turns a valve outside the cell and the water starts to flow just sort of everywhere. The cell is designed as one big wet room. Even the mattress is plastic. Just as well, because it is getting splashed. I extend a hand to check the water, more out of habit than any real desire to get naked in front of him in this big room of cages.

"It's cold."

It's more than cold. It's outright icy, the same way his eyes are. The first time I met him, he seemed like a big, cheerful Norse guy. Okay, maybe not cheerful but at least reasonably pleasant. Now he seems like the embodiment of cold cruelty.

I can't take it. It's been a really bad day, even by my standards. But I draw the line at this. I sit down on the bed which is basically just a plank with a scratchy blanket on it, and I just... stop.

I've done this once or twice in my life before. It's like I go away from myself. The world keeps going. I keep going. But

I'm not really there. I don't respond to anything. I don't do anything. I just...

Thor

There's something wrong with her. I can tell by the blank stare on her pretty face, the vacancy of her normally vibrant eyes. I've pushed her too far.

"Faen," I curse to myself. I should turn the water off and leave her where she is until she snaps out of this dissociative state. She will, eventually. Knowing her, this is probably a trick.

But I can't just walk away. Even though I want to, and even though it is what she deserves. My hammer is back in my possession, and now so is she. I don't intend on letting either of them go.

"Clean yourself up," I say.

She doesn't move. She just sits there, covered in the detritus of her victim. I forget, sometimes, that normal people, whatever that phrase means, have breaking points. I saw Bryn's young wife reach hers, and now I am afraid I have caused this girl to hit hers. We claim to protect the innocent, but it has never escaped me how much innocence we destroy.

This, however, has to be on her. She stole my hammer and taunted me. She engaged in deception and greed and she... she's shaking like a leaf.

She doesn't deserve a warm shower. She deserves a cold, harsh dose of reality. So why am I opening the door of her cell and lifting her out? Why aren't I leaving her to sob on the floor like she deserves? Why am I coating myself in

DNA and guilt and taking her upstairs to my own personal bathroom?

I tell myself it is because I am a gentleman, but really, it is because I feel sorry for her. She's pitiful. Completely out of her depth. She thought she was stealing a pretty trinket and instead she has changed the course of her life forever.

She's going to have to have a bath. She doesn't have the self-possession to take a shower. I suppose I do not blame her. What she has done is terrible beyond words and it breaks stronger men who are more prepared than she.

I have yet to tell anybody she is here. I do not think they imagined I'd actually find her when I went to look for her. I didn't think I would either, to be fair.

Fortunately, I do not encounter anybody on the stairway I choose to take up, one of the quieter ones in the West Wing of the abbey. The worst thing that could happen right now would be to run into Nina with a blood-covered, near-catatonic girl in my arms. It might tip her over the edge again, and then we'll have two damaged angels in our possession.

Looking down at this misfit, the term angel is a misnomer. She's a little devil, if anything.

My room at the abbey has an ensuite, which is nicer because it means I have a place to clean up murderous dates. Once she's safely contained in the privacy of my bathroom, I sit her on the edge of the bath and strip her of her clothing. She likes tight, black, bloody things, though the blood is generally secondary to the entire experience.

She struggles, making soft little sounds of complaint, but ultimately allows me to get her undressed. She's too overwhelmed to put up a real front of resistance. Her naked form is adorable and delicious. She's soft and curvy in all the right places. Generously built and not made for the sort of heinous acts she's just undertaken. I cannot help but admire her. She is nubile and inviting. She wraps her arms around herself, hiding parts of herself unsuccessfully. She can't hide the marks on her arse, though. The welts are still very much in evidence, little spots where the birch branch met her deserving flesh. I should have thrashed her harder and kept her then, even if Bryn tried to stop me. Letting her go back out into the world was a mistake on many levels.

"It's going to be okay," I murmur. Dammit. I am comforting her. I'm not supposed to be comforting her. She's still semi-catatonic. Dissociated. The bath should help to bring her back.

I lift her up and put her in the bath. She's adorably naked. Soft and curvy and perfect. Before I can run a bath, I have to shower her off, but she can sit there for that, while I tease gray matter out of her curls.

Soon I have hot water coursing over her, warming her, and sending little bits of man down the drain. I attempt conversation while I work to distract from the ongoing grisliness of the situation.

"What's your name?"

"Astrid," she mumbles.

"Pretty name. Norse name," I add.

"Yeah," she says. "Wait. My name's Anita. I was going to lie to you. Tell you it was Astrid. I don't know why."

"Because you're a liar."

"That's probably why," she agrees.

She's a funny little wretch. It takes everything I have not to snort with laughter. I do have some pity for her, even though I don't want to. This is exactly the kind of personality the hammer is drawn to, reckless, bold, brave, and with an incredibly limited understanding of consequences. The weapon chooses its wielder. Very few people understand that. They like to imagine that they are in control, that they have preferences, and that they are making choices. What absolute nonsense. People are acted upon, blown in the wind, and what little choice they have is usually perverted to the point it is made absolutely useless.

But enough of my philosophizing. I have a girl to wash, evidence to destroy.

With the worst of the once human goo safely down the plug hole and off to marinate and slowly decay with the rest of the Brotherhood's waste, I can run a bath for the thief.

I insert the plug and she sits patiently, letting the warm water fill up around her. She's very quiet now that she's naked and contained. Her face is flushed with shame. She's hiding from me under her curls, keeping her head down, but there is too much of her exposed for her to truly hide.

This girl is mine now. Her guilt makes her belong to me. She has abdicated all the power of an independent, law-abiding woman, and she has become my captive little sinner.

As I suspected, the warmth of the bath helps to bring her back to herself.

"Hell," she says, letting her fingers run through the water. "I've really fucked up, haven't I."

"Yes." I hand her the soap. "Get cleaned up."

She lets the soap slip from between her fingers and slide into the bath. "What's the point?"

"The point is that today is not the last day. There will be tomorrow, and the next day. And you will have to atone for your sins sooner or later, and probably again and again. That is how the worst crimes work. They create a debt that must be paid for one's entire life."

"I guess his bill is settled then, whoever that was. I did him a favor, maybe."

"Unlikely. The bill is not settled upon death, it remains with the soul."

"You are not making me feel better."

"I am not trying to make you feel better. I am trying to make you understand what a significant and unfixable mistake you have made."

She splashes me with the bathwater. It's not a playful action. It's a tearful one. "I'm sorry," she says. "I'm sorry I took your fucking hammer. And I'm more sorry I cracked someone's skull with it, but I guess I can't tell him that, can I?"

"It is too late for apologies to either one of us."

She starts to cry again. I want to thrash her. I want to chastise her so thoroughly she is completely humiliated and humbled. But for now, she is traumatized and that is not a frame of mind I can use.

So instead of beating her to within an inch of her helpless little life, I wash her. I have to dip into the bath to get the soap she lost, but I am soon using it to clean her, touching every part of her deliciously naked body with careful, and even reverent caresses. She is curvy and she is soft. There is something so delicate about her, the way she sits in the bath with her full breasts pressing against her gently rolled stomach.

She's sitting with her knees drawn up, her head down, her arms wrapped around her lower legs. I have to unfurl her gently like a flower, teasing her hands free of their grip and lowering her legs. She has dark curling down at the apex of her thighs. I spread them under the guise of washing her and find my fingers tracing up the length of them.

There's no resistance from this bright, terrible, lovely, awful woman. Just a soft moan I am sure she did not intend for me to hear. I no longer know if I am cleaning her, caressing her, or trying to seduce her. The latter seems unnecessary. She's mine. She will yield to me because that is the way of things.

I didn't intend on being this intimate this quickly, but ultimately, I made the choice to allow the hammer out of my sight and subsequently lose it. One could say this is my fault. If you extrapolate that, you could even say that what has happened to little Anita here is also my fault. But that seems like a little too much blame for my liking. So I wash her, and I consider that I might offer some words of comfort after all.

"It won't ever leave you," I repeat. "But it will lessen over time and become something you can learn from."

"What's the lesson? Don't bash people in the head with a hammer? I already fucking knew that, didn't I?"

"Don't steal. Don't lie. And do as you are told when I tell you what to do."

"Are you planning on telling me what to do?"

"Yes," I tell her. "Very much so. From this day forth. You don't take a breath I don't sanction. You took my hammer. Now I am taking you."

Anita

He means it. He really means it. I felt it when he first took me over his lap. He is possessive. He was mad I took a priceless artifact and relic, but I think he would have been mad if I'd taken his pencil. He's that sort of man.

Now I have become one of his things.

"What are you smirking about?" He gives me a dark stare. I know I should keep my mouth shut. But I can't help myself. I just have to give him shit.

"Given it took me about two minutes to steal your hammer, I'm not worried about being kidnapped by you. You're kind of careless."

He growls.

I laugh.

Another stupid decision, but it is very funny to me, even in my naked and traumatized state. Pointing out his flaws is much more enjoyable than confronting mine, that's for sure.

"You brat," he growls again. His big hands stop caressing me with warmth and care and instead take a firm grasp of my limbs.

Thor

I fish her out of the bath and bend her, wet and naked, over the curved rim. She braces herself against the floor with both hands. Good instincts. That leaves her ass for me to handle, two cheeks to punish. I start spanking her, the way I wanted to from the beginning. The way I wanted to the moment I saw her running down the street with my fucking hammer.

I don't like how good it looked in her hands. I like even less the fact that the heavens opened up as she took life. Events have now been set in motion that are impossible to undo. She's killed, and she's done it with a sacred object. She has bonded with it, and in bonding with my hammer, she has bonded with me.

She doesn't know it yet, but she cannot leave me. Not ever. We are connected now, bound by blood. Her victim has made her my thing. Forever.

Her squeals soon rise as my slaps fall. Her toes, still inside the bath, make the water splash all over the floor. The sloshing of water and the wails of the deserving woman, and the steady slaps of my flesh against hers are satisfying, but they are also sad. She doesn't know all she's given up. She has no comprehension of what she will now become. I am spanking her over the welts of my warning, a warning she did not heed.

She was already pleasantly pink from the warm water. Now her rear is bright red and getting redder with every single stroke.

"Mine. You are MINE." I snarl down at her, as if I can spank this simple and irrefutable truth into her rebellious mind.

"OW!" she shouts back. It is very hard to be coherent when one is in pain. I know that all too well. I am going to ensure that this hurts. I want her to remember this thrashing even better than the one I gave her before, the one that apparently did very little to tame her.

I spank harder. Longer. With little to nothing in the way of mercy. There is nobody to intervene now. Her cries can echo from here until...

"What the Hell!"

The door flies open and nearly off its hinges. Bryn bursts into the bathroom, unsheathed sword in one hand. He stops and he stares. We do much the same. For an extended and frankly awkward period of time, we all just look at one another.

"Can we help you?" It's Anita who breaks the silence with a sassy comment that she really shouldn't be capable of if she was in any way properly chastised. I don't know if I am actually capable of spanking this girl enough to teach her a lesson. I don't know if anybody is. She should be in floods of tears and begging for mercy, and instead she is talking to Bryn as if he's the one being inappropriate.

"I heard a woman screaming," he explains.

"Oh my god, get the fuck out!" Anita shouts at him.

He looks at her, narrow eyed, before probably realizing there is no way his bride would be happy with him looking at a naked wench. He backs out of the room, shutting the door behind him.

"Thor! I'd like to speak with you as soon as is convenient," he announces through the wood.

"Certainly," I reply. "I just need to finish up with this one."

"I'm sore," she says as we listen to Bryn's footsteps receding. "Could you possibly finish beating me later, maybe after I have had something to eat?"

She's part punk princess, part Dickensian waif. I don't think she's had an easy life. Her talent for opportunism and her particular lack of moral fiber represent the character traits gained through hardship.

Bryn's interruption has given me a moment to consider what I am doing, and who I am doing it to. I want to teach her an immediate lesson once and for all, but realistically, that is not how this sort of thing works. If she learns at all, it is most likely going to be a slow and painful process for us both.

Picking her up, I stop spanking her and instead turn my attention to patting her dry. She has the sense to hold her tongue long enough for that to happen. I am sure that she is not used to being washed and dried, but I take care of what is mine. I like how she feels close to me. I like how warm she is. I like her natural scent, which still hangs about the roots of her hair and behind her earlobes.

My hammer is with me, right where it should be, hanging at my waist. The shaft fits through a particularly shaped loop on my belt, and the head holds it in place.

"What are you doing?"

I'm taking it from my waist, and I am running the sheath under the water, with soap. This is not how I usually clean the hammer. Usually, I polish and sand and perhaps seal it, but for now I want it clean enough to do something suitably twisted.

"Hands and knees," I order. "Your punishment begins now."

A little whimper marks her attempt to avoid her comeuppance, but she has to know that a little spanking is not nearly enough. She needs to be sorer, more deeply embarrassed. She needs to feel true regret and contrition. She needs the shaft of my hammer buried deep in her...

"Oh fuck!" She curses as she feels the hard but smoothly curved end of the hammer running along the length of her slit. It is built sturdily, a lot thicker than the average cock, but not so thick she can't take it in this naughty pussy.

I make her stretch for me. I press it between those tender lips of hers, watching them spread for me. She's a little brat, a true hellion, and this is how I show my things their place.

"Thor..."

I love the way her voice catches and cracks. I love the way she is braced even more. She may not wish for this, but she is pressing back against it, she is taking my long, hard hammer in her tight little cunt now. I feel the moment it breaches the last point of resistance and begins to simply slide in, gliding on her wet humiliation.

She grunts and moans, her round hips working back and forth against the shaft.

"This is wrong," she gasps. "I stole this. I..."

"Quiet," I order. This is no longer about what she has done. This is what is being done to her. She is being obedient. She is opening herself up. She is taking what she deserves, a good fucking following a hard spanking. My cock is rock hard inside my pants, but as tempted as I am to drive that inside her hot cunt, I think this holds so much more meaning for her.

Harder. Faster. Deeper. I pump my hammer in and out of her until she is on the verge of a very undeserved orgasm, and at that moment I pull it out, ignoring her begging. She wants to orgasm. She thinks she has earned pleasure. But this is not about her pleasure or her dripping need. It is about teaching the little animal part of her a lesson it will never forget.

"You have another hole equally in need of fucking," I remind her.

"No!"

"Yes."

"No!"

"Yes. Hold your cheeks open for me."

This is a test of obedience. She cannot stay on hands and knees if she is to hold herself open for me. She must instead lower her cheek to the floor and present her haunches high, two red swelling globes on either side of a dark little hole I am yet to conquer, and the dripping slit I have already claimed with my hammer.

The sounds she makes as I use the ample slick lubrication from her sex to ease the passage of my hammer's shaft into her tight rectum are some of the most satisfying I will ever hear. Her little gasps, moans, and complaints are music to my ears. I think back to how smart she was when she was calling me, taunting me with her possession of this very hammer. She has it now, pressing into the tightness of her rear.

"Is this what you wanted? When you called me and told me you had my hammer? When you tried to take thousands of pounds from me? Or when you swore I'd never get it back? Do you remember that, Anita?"

"Yessss!" Her moans are deeper and more desperate. She's losing control, what little she had left. She's giving into those baser impulses and instincts that lie at the core of every red-blooded woman. She's taking her fucking like a good girl — and it may very well be the only thing she ever does as a good girl.

"It's mine again now, isn't it. And so are you."

"Yes!"

I reach between her legs and toy with that dripping sex that calls me. I could pull my hammer free and plunge my cock into her. I could feel her wrap around me with all that desperate intensity I know she has. She'd love my cock inside her. But she doesn't deserve that. She deserves this. The shaft of my hammer gliding in and out of her hottest, tightest hole, urging her anally toward what I hope to make the most memorable orgasm of her life.

She's getting closer. Her thighs are shaking with desperate need. She can barely keep her bottom still, her fingers struggling to keep her cheeks spread. But she obeys, and because she obeys, she is allowed to orgasm.

"Come for me," I order gruffly, pinching the nub of her clit between my fingers and rubbing it back and forth as much as that filthy little bud can take.

She cannot hold back. Not for a second. She comes with an animal scream, trembling and writhing. I pull the shaft free before she does herself any damage and watch as she collapses onto the bathroom floor, her fingers delving between her thighs to greedily drag the last vestiges of pleasure from the moment. She is wise to do so.

"Hands off," I order, standing over her. She'll soon learn that she gets nothing I have not allowed her.

I have fucked her into submission. I have used the very tool she has sinned with to shame and castigate her. And I have driven myself to the point of being nearly unable to stand with the aching in my balls, but that is a small price to pay for the message I have sent. We were filthy and debased, and I enjoyed every moment of it. By the look of her flushed face, I think she did too — even the parts she wasn't supposed to.

I have driven myself half-mad with need for her, but of course I cannot merely follow rough instinct. Bryn will want an explanation, and I need enough blood running to my brain to be able to fabricate one.

"Get up and dry yourself," I tell her, tossing a towel over her.

She catches it and shoots me a look of temper. That did not take long to return. A woman such as this does not stay in the state of submission for long.

"I have nothing to wear," she says, scrambling up from the floor and wrapping the towel about her body. "My other clothes are covered in German man."

How quickly practical concerns overshadow these moments of intense intimacy. My clothes will not fit her, obviously. But I do find a shirt that will suffice as a dress for her.

"Really. You expect me to wear this?" She holds it by the collar. It will be far too large, but the white shirt will do the job.

"It's the only thing I have that will cover you, and you will want to be dressed, I assume."

"I don't want to see Bryn," she says. "Not after."

"And you're not going to. I'm going to take you to the kitchen, and I am going to introduce you to a woman who is not, under any circumstances, to be crossed. Do you understand? Mrs Crocombe is to be respected. Not only because she is a lady who works very hard for this household, but because she is where the food comes from. Understand?"

She tosses her head and shoots me a look of such impertinence it is hard to believe she just knelt and held herself open for a good anal fucking. "Yes. I understand basic English."

I spank her exposed bottom as she attempts to clothe herself. She makes a little yelp and rises to her toes. She has the cutest toes.

"You might understand the words, but you certainly do not understand the meaning," I growl.

She is going to need constant handling, this one. I cannot wait.

Anita

I am aching, inside and out, physically and mentally. He made me come so fucking hard I almost forgot my name — and I'm in the mood to forget, so that was a favor.

This big Viking is even more twisted than I imagined. He's harsh and he's a little bit cruel in a way I think I like. I know I deserve a lot worse than what he just did to me. But I also know what he just did was wrong.

It's hard to meet his eyes now. I don't bother. That throwaway comment just got me smacked hard enough to not want to try another one. I am in real trouble. Life changing trouble.

But for now, it sounds like I am going to be fed, and that's all I need to understand. I can forgive and forget a lot of things in exchange for a hot meal. Like the hammer murder I perpetrated, and the absolute lashing Thor has given me. I am so fucking sore, but I am even more hungry.

I finish putting the shirt on. It barely covers my arse, but that's probably a merciful thing. This man loves to punish. He takes glee in it, I think. When his palm was thundering down against my skin, I could feel him getting harder and harder against my hip and thigh. He's a sadist. And he's something more than that too. The hammer isn't a replica of anything. It's real. It has power. Yes, any hammer can crush a skull, but I felt real power coursing through me. I felt the hammer's essence all the way inside me. It felt like... him.

He thinks I talk too much, but I'm not saying even half of what I'm thinking. I haven't worked this out fully yet. I don't know quite who he is... or what he is. He's not a normal man, that's for certain.

Thor takes me by the hand and leads me out of his room. The abbey is just as I expected it to be. Old. Run down. Gothic in the extreme. This is a place that needs millions put into it to get it back to its old self. I can feel the energies here. I imagine anybody could.

"Mrs Crocombe?" Thor calls out to a kindly lady in the kitchen. She has graying hair and a floral apron and she's bustling about between more pots and pans than I can imagine anybody needs to cook basically anything.

"Yes! How can I help you, young man?" She comes toward us with a smile.

"This is Anita. She's going to be staying here for some time. As in, she's not allowed to leave. I was hoping you could feed her and keep an eye on her. I'm sure she'll be good for you, because there will be hell to pay if she isn't."

"Of course I can. What do you like to eat, Anita?"

"Literally anything," I reply. "This all smells amazing."

A broad smile crosses her face. "Then I wager we are going to get on very well indeed. Come and sit down."

"I'll leave you two," Thor says. "Please, Mrs Crocombe, call me if you have any problems."

"I'm sure that won't be necessary," she says.

"I'm not so sure," he says, cutting me a severe glare. One might think he'd soften after everything we've just done, but apparently soft is not in his vocabulary. I thought punishment was supposed to lead to forgiveness. I suppose I haven't been punished enough yet.

"Pie," Mrs Crocombe says. "Come sit at the kitchen table and have a slice."

"I can't sit," I say ruefully once he's gone. "But this really looks delicious."

"Well, you won't be the first lass to eat standing up in this kitchen, and I'd very much doubt you being the last."

I like her. She has a warmth about her and a no-nonsense attitude. She is also generous with her portions, feeding me like I am starving. The more I eat, the better I feel about life in general. The aching in my arse is starting to fade to a dull throb, but the stretched sensation inside is going to stay with me some time longer, I imagine.

What a twisted fucker he is.

7

Thor

"Got your hammer back, I see."

Bryn is going for understatement for now. I'm certain he'd like to curse and break things. I'm almost certain he's broken something already. This is starting to get messy, and to no benefit for him.

"Yes. Not without cost."

"Yes. You appear to have the girl as well."

"I do."

The conversation is a little stilted and awkward, but really, we have all seen more and worse than what he just saw. We are brothers, and that means a certain intimacy that comes with being family.

"You shouldn't have brought her back here, Thor."

"I had to."

"Why?"

"Because she killed someone with the hammer."

His brows rise almost all the way to the dark shock of hair threatening to fall into them. Bryn is master of Direview Abbey by birth, and the local parish priest besides, but he is not a traditionally groomed priest. None of us are particularly traditional in any way.

The news that Anita has murdered somebody does not strike him the way it might be expected to. He does not give into hysterics or righteous condemnation. After a moment, his brows return to their usual locations.

"Well," he says. "And what are we going to do about that?"

"She's mine now."

"Yes. I suppose she has to be."

"Nonsense!" There's a general harrumphing from the direction of the fire. I didn't notice Steven asleep there, the oldest of the Brotherhood, and the wisest of us all.

"Call the police and turn the little hammer murderer in," Steven says, spluttering awake. His mood has not improved lately. I wonder if he needs a tune up of his arthritis medications. Old people need a lot of medical maintenance.

"I don't want to do that, and when you hear where the murder happened, neither will you."

"Where did it happen?" Bryn asks.

"Craig's house."

"How does she know Craig?" Bryn asks another very good question. Questions I might have asked if I was not so obsessed with dominating and claiming her. It is time she was interrogated.

"Oh. By the way. Her name is Anita."

"Anita..."

"I don't know her last name."

"Well. It is hard to get to know someone when you have them naked, wet, and upside down." Bryn smirks. "Bring her to us."

"She's not exactly dressed at the moment. I didn't catch her with a spare change of clothes. Does Nina have anything that'll work?"

"Nina!" Bryn calls his wife's name.

After a minute or two, Nina appears. She looks bored. I don't like that look. Boredom is one of the most dangerous moods that can take a woman or a man, but especially a woman. Women do not like ruts. We enjoy them, as a general rule. Same thing day after day, never changing, that sounds fine to me. But Nina is almost twenty-one, and once she gets over her many traumas, she will be looking for adventure. Or worse — babies.

"Yeah?" Nina's American slang could be construed as disrespectful if one wanted to construe it that way. I do, but Bryn gives her leeway. A lot of leeway.

"Do you have any loose fit clothing that will fit the girl who stole Thor's hammer?"

Nina's eyes brighten. "I don't know. I think I have a track suit? Or maybe some of Jonah's old things if she doesn't mind smelling of boy?"

"Give it to Thor; he can go dress the prisoner."

"You're keeping someone prisoner? Why?" Nina is immediately curious.

"No reason," I say, thinking the topic hardly suitable for Nina.

"She brained someone with a hammer," Bryn says.

"Wow."

Wow indeed. Wow. Wow. Wow.

"I'll get the tracksuit," she says. "It's very 2008, which I guess makes now two thousand and late, but I was going through a stage and I think it'll fit."

~

"I got you some clothes," I tell Anita. My shirt is fine for eating in the kitchen with Crocombe, but not suitable for an audience with the Brotherhood. I don't know that what I have in hand will be any better, but it is pink and soft. I'm given to understand girls generally like that sort of thing, but perhaps not this girl. Her typical clothes are all black with shiny bits, studs and things. I'm sure she's going to scoff at...

Her eyes light up unexpectedly. "Is that velour?"

"I believe so."

"Wow."

The abbey has a new word of the day, and apparently that is it.

She takes it and does that thing women do when they hold clothing to their body rather than just put it on. I'm not sure what purpose that serves, but it seems to please her. "This is nice. Soft! Thank you!"

"You can thank Nina. She's lent it to you."

"Who is Nina?"

"Bryn's wife?"

"That cunt is married?"

I find myself laughing at her bluntness before I can regroup. "Put it on," I say. "Before you get yourself into any more trouble."

She dresses in the kitchen. The tracksuit does look a little odd with her boots, but she doesn't seem to care about that. It's also a bit long and snug in the places she is more generously built, but it works. Overall, the tracksuit looks like an older item of clothing, well worn. Nice of Nina to share it. My knowledge of women tells me that it is either a favorite, or something she'd not be seen dead in.

Anita cranes her head over her shoulder. "Why does my ass say 'juicy' right now?"

"You should be glad that's all your ass says," I growl. "Come with me. You have some explaining to do."

"To who?"

"To Bryn and another priest named Steven."

. . .

A*nita*

"Why do I give a fuck what they think? You want to take me to the police, fine. I don't give a toss about these wankers in dresses."

Food has renewed my energy and my lip. Yes, I still physically ache, but I'm willing to give them some shit anyway. Thor doesn't own me, even if he thinks he does.

"Because you are trouble, and Direview is home to us all. They need to know what kind of dilemma you are going to pose. I need to know what happened too. It's best we all discover that together."

"Fine. Not like I have any choice, do I?"

"No. You do not."

I walk my aptly described rear into the drawing room he guides me into where the priests are waiting. I really don't care about this particular interlude. I am not religious and I do not answer to them.

"This is Father Bryn; you've met him before. The older gentleman is Steven. Gentlemen, this is Anita."

I don't say hello. It's not that kind of meeting. This is a hostile room. I've been in plenty of those before. Thor is behind me, so I can't look to him for hints and direction. I keep my eyes on Bryn.

"How did you know Craig?" Father Bryn asks the question. He's sitting in a very big ornate chair with twiddly bits on the top. He looks very much in command, which I suppose is the point of big ornate chairs with twiddly bits. He doesn't need the chair. He and Thor have a similar air of natural authority. Even now, faced with Bryn, most of my attention is on Thor behind me, and I can't see him at all — except in my mind's eye.

"He used to give me free extras they were going to throw away at the supermarket. I don't make much money, so I made friends with him when he used to do the bins."

"What do you mean, made friends when he did the bins?"

"I mean he felt sorry for me when he caught me stealing from the skip. So he said if I met him at a certain time, he'd give me whatever he could. I got lots of baked stuff that way, things that had just gone out of date. I haven't bought food in a year."

"And what did he get in return?"

Now it's my turn to ask the *what do you mean* question. Sounds to me like Father Bryn is making an unsavory and completely dishonorable suggestion.

"I didn't suck dick for old noodles, if that's what you mean."

"Anita." Thor growls my name softly, and for some reason the low volume produces an even more intense reaction than yelling and smacking would have.

"What? He's implying that I'm some kind of muffin whore."

Bryn is smirking now. Even Thor is having a hard time keeping a straight face, and he is really very angry at me.

"I have her possessions here. What she had with her, anyway."

I didn't notice Thor had my rucksack. It was perched over his shoulder this whole time. It looks small on him. Everything looks small on him.

"Let's see them."

Thor tips my bag out. Several packets of noodles and a can or two of soup clunk onto the ground. Kind of a sad little haul, really. I hate the pity on their faces. I hate having people feel sorry for me.

"You've been eating out of bins, and you went to Craig's house to scavenge some more," Bryn recaps.

"Yes. But he's gone somewhere. You know where he is?"

There's a moment where everybody is uncomfortable, and I realize they definitely know something. They are collectively silently agreeing to keep me in the dark.

"He was just a harmless old guy. I called his disappearance into the cops."

"Why?" Father Bryn scowls the question at me.

"Because everybody deserves to be missed? I don't know. He was sad. Past tense is the right way to talk about him, isn't it?"

Now they're all avoiding my gaze. Father Bryn is staring at Thor, as if he's trying to pound some kind of thought into his brain

"Are you all telepathic?"

"You can take her away," Bryn says.

"Oh, so you want to talk about me and not have me listen? Shouldn't you be calling the police about me? After all, a crime has been committed, and with a magical hammer, no less. You know, it felt to me rather like the hammer was acting on its own in some way. Like, I wasn't fully in control of my actions..."

Now I am thinking out loud. Partially to annoy them, of course, but also partially to process what happened. I didn't mean to hurt anybody. I just did what I did. It was like the hammer raised my arms instead of my arms raising the hammer. But is that possible?

"A crime was committed because you do not have the power to wield the hammer," Thor growls. "It was base instinct, animal impulse that led you to act as you did. It was not the hammer's fault. My weapon does not bear blame."

"Your weapon has left some angry German man with his brain matter spread across the kitchen floor," I say, feeling better when I put it that way. "Not that it matters; if anybody tried to get prints off it now, they'd only get an arse print."

The old coot looks suitably scandalized. Bryn palms his face. He clearly intended on this meeting having more decorum, and of me being more ashamed and scared of them all — but what do I really have left to lose now?

"What happened in the house?" Bryn prompts me.

"Someone broke into Craig's house after I let myself in and was smashing it up looking for something. I heard him talking to his accomplice on the phone."

"Did you hear what they were looking for?" Bryn interjects with another question.

"No. But they were angry and impatient and swearing a lot. Seemed like they were really desperate to get it. Drugs, maybe? Craig didn't seem like the type, but does anybody?"

"I know what they were looking for," Bryn says. "You can put her back, Thor."

"What were they looking for? Who was it? What's happening? Hey! I killed someone over this. I deserve to know!"

"You deserve endless punishments of unending pain," Thor says. "Come with me."

"What's going on? Why did I just kill someone? I deserve answers!"

"You deserve a month of spankings."

"Put her down in the dungeon," Bryn says. "She's a flight risk."

∽

"You going to let him tell you what to do with me?"

I ask Thor the question as he escorts me away.

"Bryn talks to you like he's your boss," I add. "Not your brother. Do I answer to him or to you?"

"Cut it out," Thor growls. "I know what you're trying to do, and it isn't going to work."

"He walks into your bathroom, tells you where to put me. Seems to me he pisses all over your territory, mate. I'm surprised he doesn't have your hammer."

By now, we're back down in the dungeon. It is a fucking freaky place, and I don't want to be left here.

"If you guys had wanted to make real money, you should have told everybody there was a dungeon, and you'd put them in it if they were very naughty. People pay good money for that."

"You killed someone with stolen property today. Little less flippancy, please."

"It was self-defense. Whatever he was going to do to me, I don't think I would have liked, and also, the more I think about it, the more it really seems like the hammer did it."

"Is a jury going to buy that?"

"Well. I don't know. Depends how good my lawyer is, and if you testify that you're Thor, ancient god of thunder. And if the hammer itself is entered into evidence, which it would have to be or they don't actually have the weapon, which is important."

Thor picks me up again. He treats me more like a recalcitrant pet to be carried about than a person capable of walking on her own. I suppose in our brief history, me walking around has caused him no end of trouble.

"What are you going to do with me? Or to me? You can't keep me here forever. Someone will notice I'm missing. And you can't turn me in, or..."

"Quiet," he growls down at me. "I'm well aware of how much trouble you are, and how much trouble you might yet cause."

He drops me into a cell and closes the door behind me.

"Thor," I say, grasping the bars. "Please don't leave me here."

He ignores me.

~

It has been many hours and still I am whimpering to myself in the dark. I hate Thor more than I have hated anybody. He has no right to put me here, to violate my body and then to contain me. Far as I'm concerned, if someone fucks your arse with their hammer, they should let you stay in their room. Not this dark, terrifying undercroft. I don't know if that's the right word, but it is definitely the right feeling.

I hear a creak in the distance. There's a sliver of light that grows and then thins again.

Thor! He's come back for me.

I hear footsteps and try to compose myself. I don't want him to know that I have been crying. I want to keep up the appearance of being utterly emotionally untouchable.

I smell food. Smells like a fish and chip shop. My mouth begins to water and my mood starts to lift. Food and company, two things no captive can live without. Everything is going to be okay.

But it's not Thor. It is a much more refined gentleman. When he speaks, I recognize his voice from the phone. What was his name again? Did he ever tell me?

"I thought you might be hungry, miss. I've brought you something to eat." He's bought me a hot chip butty.

Common food. I'm surprised someone with an accent like his even knows what it is, let alone deigns to bring it to me in his own refined hand.

"Did Thor tell you to feed me?"

He bristles silently but visibly. "I do not need to be told to ensure that guests are well tended to."

"I am hardly a guest. More like a prisoner."

"That is a matter not in my purview. Ensuring that your basic needs are met is."

He passes the plate through a slot in the bars. I take it in both hands. I don't know what the time is, but it feels late. This will be a midnight feast to remember. I settle back down on the bed, plate on my knees, and I take the sandwich in both hands. The bread is thick and soft, homemade, I am sure. The chips are thick and hand cut, and really well fried with crunchy bits left on the ends. The first mouthful is hot and salty with that perfectly fried hint of fat that immediately satisfies and soothes.

"I never understood why they installed these infernal things," he says conversationally, running his hand up the cage that holds me. "The enemies of the Brotherhood are not ones to be confined by physical bars."

"I'm not an enemy of the Brotherhood. I don't know what the Brotherhood is."

"You have made an enemy of them yourself by your actions, I am afraid."

"So who are they? What is their deal? Obviously not simple priests and friends."

"The Brotherhood is a blood sworn order of men sworn to protect what is pure on this Earth."

It takes me a moment to reply with a mouth full of potato and bread. "They sound racist."

"The purity they seek to defend is not of this Earth. It supersedes all races, all creeds, all philosophical inclinations. It is the blood of the angels they defend."

"Wow. The blood of actual angels? And where is that?"

"Running in the veins of a blessed few."

"In me?" I sound more hopeful than I am. I already know I am no angel. Demon, maybe. Angel, definitely not.

"Not in you," he says, his lips quirking with amusement at the very idea. "You are as far from the angels as it is possible to be."

"So why are they keeping me?"

"Probably something to do with the heinous murder you recently committed, I imagine."

"Oh, yes. That."

"That," he says.

I'm starting to get more comfortable. I sit cross-legged on the bed, such as it is, and make the most of my little feast.

"This was really nice of you. You and Mrs Crocombe have been so lovely to me. And the priests have been... absolute fucking assholes."

"We recognize those who need kindness better than they do, sometimes."

"I don't think I can sleep here."

"If you do not mind me taking the liberty, I think I will stay for a while. Perhaps you will find it easier to rest then."

I almost question his niceness, but then I realize it might insult or embarrass him, and I don't want to do either of those things.

"Do you think I am a bad person? What's your name? I can't keep talking to you without knowing that, it's rude."

"My name is Edmund Crichton, and I am at your service. As for whether you are a bad person..." He pauses for a moment, gathering all his diplomacy. "You are a person, and people, generally speaking, are all bad. It's not their fault. It is merely the way they were made. Humans are flawed creatures full of desires and drives they can never physically satiate within the bounds of social proprietary."

"They don't usually do what I did today. Any of what I did today."

What a day I have had. I killed someone with a hammer and then I let another near virtual stranger fuck my bottom with that same weapon... and then I came. I'm about as twisted as they come.

"Whatever you did today... and whatever was done to you today, it is done. The fathers will attempt to instill guilt, but that is not for you."

He talks to me like he knows me, not personally, but specifically. Like there's some secret I am unaware of.

"Why isn't it for me?"

"Because you are the kind to see an artifact of power and to lay hands on it no matter what. You will not follow the rules of men, because you know somewhere inside that they were never meant for one like you."

"You should tell Thor that."

"It is not my place to tell Thor anything. I hope to offer you a little comfort in what must be a dark and trying time. Mrs Crocombe and I have spoken about you, and we have decided to aid you as best we can. Direview Manor has not historically been a happy place for young women."

"That's nice of you," I say, because it is. My eyes are starting to feel heavy. A yawn begins to escape me. I lie down just for a moment, to rest.

8

Anita

Never thought I'd sleep in a cell, but I did.

With Crichton outside the bars, the dark was transformed from the terrifying solitary unknown to the warm and surprisingly cozy kind of dark.

I am now curled up under a scratchy military blanket in the dungeon. I wake up with my hands curled around something hard and warm, something that throbs against me. I am so cozy. So happy. There are things at the edges of my memory trying to push into my happy just-woken-up state, but I'm keeping them away for now and focusing on the simple joys of drifting between awake and not awake.

Crichton is no longer there; he has disappeared to bring comfort to some other captive, perhaps. That's okay. I have made it through the night, and I feel better for it. Sleep restores more than the body. It clears the mind.

"It's missing again!" Someone's shouting upstairs. Thor, I think. His voice has a very particular thundering quality that makes it difficult to ignore. It goes right through me, vibrating against the jelly parts and the not so jelly parts too. I am still gently aching from yesterday, and now I am blushing with the memory of punishment and pleasure.

I can hear feet pounding the old floor boards above. Judging by the way they crack and creak and let dust of god knows what outlawed compounds fall down here in a shimmering haze, it won't just be the roof that needs replacing soon. This whole place is slowly falling apart — except the dungeon. This has been renovated to within an inch of its life. The money in this place has been spent on what is hidden and what is wrong.

They come downstairs, Thor and Bryn. Light streams in through the dungeon door. It occurs to me that this place needs some more men in it. Two of them to search the whole place every time they lose something is just inefficient, even with the two staff.

The two of them come charging up to my cell. Thor's so large he makes Bryn look like his son. That's an amusing thought that ensures I am smirking and composed by the time they arrive at my bars.

"Where is it?" Thor growls the question at me.

"I literally just woke up. I have no idea what the fuck you are talking about."

"The hammer. My hammer."

"I don't know! I've been locked in this cage alone all night!"

"She's right," Thor says to Bryn. "There's no way..."

"Then what is that?" Bryn points to a lump beneath the blanket, right where I am curled up. I don't know what it is. I haven't exactly had a lot of looking around time.

"My dick?" I offer the explanation. Nobody finds it amusing besides me, but that's not a unique experience. I tell jokes others don't find amusing all the time.

Thor opens the door. It's funny, because it takes him longer than it should. He keeps fumbling with the keys out of annoyance. Finally, he gets the door open and grabs the blanket off me.

I do have his hammer. Again.

"My hammer!" Thor growls at me. He takes it from me, fisting it in one hand. For me, it's a two-hand kind of deal. For him, it almost looks like a toy. It's strange how such a small and generally unassuming thing can be so powerful.

Before he can start throwing accusations at me, I start defending myself. "I didn't steal it! How could I have stolen it? I've been locked up! It must have creeped in here overnight."

"That's not possible."

"The other possibility is that I can escape this cage and I'm still here. Which makes less sense than your magic god hammer magicking itself here. I am feeling even less responsible for that murder thing now. It's like a weight has been lifted."

He hesitates, for just a second. That makes me smile. He's slightly worried about the hammer too, I think. It has come to me of its own free will, and he knows it. I'm starting to really wonder who the hell this guy is. If he is a god, then he has little to fear. If he is a man with an artifact he doesn't understand, then he risks death by thwarting its will, because I am more certain than ever that this prize is none other than Mjollnir, hammer of Actual Thor. AT, for short.

"Thor's hammer likes me better than it likes him," I smirk. "Me and Mjoll are friends."

"What?" Thor laughs. "You think this is that hammer?"

"Sure. Why not. Looks like Thor's hammer. The real Thor, I mean. Not you, Thor Larsen. Man who keeps losing it."

That makes him snarl all the more. "You don't know what you're getting involved with, you little shit. You've killed a man through your involvement with this cursed thing. Did it ever occur to you that there might be more than one sentient tool in the world?"

"Most of the men I've dated have been sentient tools, so, yes."

"Very funny," he deadpans.

I thought it actually was very funny, but you don't get half the credit for humor when you're a woman who has just killed someone.

"You don't know what you have, and you don't know why it is choosing you," Thor says. "You understand nothing, because you have just read a few sanitized histories and neutered myths. There is real evil in the world. True darkness of the kind that can and will swallow you whole. And you have come tangential to something more powerful than you can contain. It will not lift you up. It will ultimately destroy you."

"And you had this shit out on a fete!"

"Bad idea, in retrospect," he agrees.

"Bad idea in any kind of spect."

He sighs. "You need to be separated from it. You need to be sent somewhere."

Why do I feel slightly disappointed about that? Oh, right, because here I was all warm and my room was secure, and there was the best food ever in the kitchen. The cell that scared me now feels quite cozy.

"What if I don't want to go?"

"You can't stay."

"Why not?"

"Well, this is an abbey and you're not one of the Brotherhood. Also you're an arsonist, a thief, and at least an accessory to murder."

"Seems dangerous to let me roam around Direford, doesn't it? And what if I told someone about the dungeon up here? And all the..."

"Alright. Shut up," he growls

I have the feeling the hammer is going to come back to me one way or another anyway. But I play along for now. He's not happy with me. His expression is thunderous. Suddenly, I don't know that coming out of the cage is the best idea.

"If you want to be tolerated here, don't touch anything that's not yours. So, anything. And don't set anything on fire or I will whip you from now until the end of time." He swings the door open and I step out. "Get upstairs," he says. "You know where the kitchen is already, go and ask Mrs Crocombe for some food. If you're lucky, she'll feed you."

"And if I'm not?"

"She'll chase you out of her kitchen and make you wait until dinner time."

I leave the cell, walking between the angry Thor and strangely silent Bryn before dashing up the stairs for breakfast.

Thor

Bryn and I exchange unhappy looks.

Keeping the hammer in my possession is harder than it seems. It has an affinity for Anita, but it cannot grow legs and walk, of course. That means it was delivered. We both know the only entity likely to have done that.

"Crichton!" Bryn shouts for his manservant.

The demon butler appears.

"Why did you move the hammer from Thor's possession to the girl's?"

Crichton's expression barely shifts as he is accused. However, he makes the matter slightly easier by not denying his role in the affair.

"It wishes to be with her. She has fed the spirit. It was crying out for her all night long, and finally I could stand the infernal din no more, sir. I apologize."

"You realize she could have used that weapon against any one of us?"

"Sleep is a blessed mercy," Crichton replies, ignoring the inference.

"I am beginning to think that you are not as much on my side as I might like, Crichton," Bryn continues.

"I take great offense to that, sir. I am doing what needs to be done, even if those actions are not apparent to you in the moment. I have always acted in the best interests of this house and its inhabitants. Let the hammer sleep with the girl and let the girl sleep with the god. All will sleep well."

"I am not a god," I say, hotly.

"Yes, sir. Very good, sir." Crichton agrees far too smoothly.

"I am not a god," I repeat to Bryn.

"I know. I've seen you bleed. But you used to have that thing under control, and you don't anymore. The sliver of power in you is waning, perhaps. Or the girl has a stronger one inside her."

"Not possible."

We call this ability of mine a sliver of the ancient because saying that I have some old Norse power inside me would really throw a spanner in the proverbial works, given we are both ostensibly Anglican priests.

"She needs to be told," Bryn said. "She needs to understand why the thing is so drawn to her, and why she is capable of atrocity when she wields it. It's not enough to take it from her. It's going to come back. And it's not enough to punish her in a bathroom. She has sinned, Thor. She has sinned against man and against god using an infernal weapon that should not be tolerated to exist."

Bryn would be more comfortable if we destroyed the hammer, but I don't think it can be destroyed. The physical form of the thing could be broken, but the hammer is not a thing. It is a being. A force that commands those near it to do its will. There is no point berating Crichton. He did the hammer's bidding obediently, just as Anita did. I am the one who thwarts the unseen beast. But I made a mistake. I let years of calm lull me into believing the hammer was just an artifact. It fooled me, and now that it has tasted blood, it cries out for more.

9

Anita

"Mrs Crocombe?" I say her name hopefully. Thor seems to be a little afraid of the woman, but I think she's lovely. Yesterday she brought me the first comfort I've felt in a long time. There can be no overestimating the value of a warm kitchen and fresh baking.

"Oh, hey!" Nina smiles. She's already in the kitchen eating breakfast. Croissants and strawberries await, a better breakfast than I have indulged in for a very long time.

"Hey," I reply. "Thanks for the lend of the tracksuit."

"No problem. You can come pick through my closet if you like."

"That's really nice, but I'm hoping I can get my own things soon. Assuming Thor lets me out of the house."

"Bryn rarely lets me out," she commiserates. "Unless I am going to church."

"So you're a prisoner too? How many girls are stuck here with these old creeps?"

Nina smirks around her croissant. "Just us," she says. "Eat something. You'll need your strength to run when they hear you calling them old creeps."

"Shoe fits," I say, grabbing three of the croissants. One goes in my mouth. The other two each go into the pockets of the tracksuit. Nina gives me a weird look. She's a beautiful girl. Elegant. One of those people who probably floats through life being stunningly tragic. But she's never had to hoard food, and it shows.

She doesn't say anything as I sit down to eat.

Mrs Crocombe comes bustling in, wiping her hands on a tea towel stuck into the ties of the floral apron around her waist.

"Morning, Mrs Crocombe," I say.

"Oh, it's you," she says with a smile. "Hope you weren't too cold down there in those awful cells."

"What awful cells?" Nina frowns.

"There's cells in the dungeon. I stayed in one last night because..."

"Because why?" Her pretty green eyes are wide and fascinated.

"Because I killed a guy."

"Eat up!" Mrs Crocombe declares, placing a fresh plate of croissants between us, as well as a plate of sausages, eggs, and bacon. I didn't even see her cook those. It is my turn for my eyes to go wide. This is more food in one place than I think I have ever seen except in one of those buffet restaurants where budget-conscious diners play roulette with E. coli infections from handsy small people.

"You are too kind," I say. "This is amazing."

She seems very pleased at my appreciation.

"I'd happily spend every night in a cell if this was breakfast every morning," I say.

"Why are you sleeping in a cell?" Nina repeats the question.

"Murder, remember?"

"Oh. Right. Yes. Sorry. You did tell me. Why did you murder someone?"

"I am fairly certain he was going to murder me if I didn't murder him first. I don't know, of course, but I had a feeling that was how it was going to go."

"Oh. Well. That's alright then, isn't it?"

She seems a little spacey sometimes, like she's in two worlds at once and the rest of us are only privy to one of them. I am curious about her. I've never seen her down in the village. Kind of seems as though she is as much of a prisoner as I am.

"So you married Bryn? What are you? Twenty? He's got to be forty. What makes an American come here and marry... oh. Never mind. I get it."

Bryn's just walked in shirtless. They say age is just a number, and that's not true, but holy hell, those abs and that face. He looks like a vengeful demon himself. The hot kind.

The only hotter one here is Thor. I'm glad she didn't marry him. Went for Mr Tall, Dark, and Growly instead.

Bryn spots Nina first. I see a smile spread over his face, a sweet expression of love and affection. Then he sees me and that expression fades immediately.

"What are you doing..." he trails off. He doesn't want to finish that sentence, apparently. Maybe Nina here doesn't know there's a whole underground prison here. She strikes me as the type clinging to the last remnants of innocence. I don't imagine it lasts long here. Mine has been shattered six ways from Sunday. "I don't think the two of you should be talking."

He thinks I am a bad influence. That's cute.

"Why not?" Nina asks the question sweetly, not petulantly.

"Well, one of you murdered someone recently and the other is my wife."

"I'm bored," Nina says. "She's nice. The hammer thing sounds like an accident."

"I will whip you both if you get into a hint of trouble," Bryn promises. "And then Thor will have you again, Anita. Understand?"

I've never had this much personal attention from authority figures before. It's kind of exciting. I'm used to slipping through the cracks and going unnoticed. But that's not exactly going to happen here.

"I'm on my best behavior," I promise him. That makes Nina laugh. I don't know why.

"What?"

"When you say that, you sound like you're lying."

I'm not lying, weirdly. I'm telling the truth. This place is basically a jail I'm choosing to stay in. If I wanted to be gone, I could have walked out the front door just now instead of coming up for breakfast.

Bryn sighs. "Just... don't do anything stupid." He's looking at me, not at Nina.

"I just came for breakfast. Like I was told to. I don't want any trouble."

He growls and continues on his way, back through the kitchen down to some other part of the dungeon. I wonder if there are more cells down there.

"Your husband doesn't like me," I comment to Nina. I don't know if she likes me either, strictly speaking. But I am the only other person under thirty in the household and a girl.

"He doesn't like anybody who might hurt me," she says. "He's got good reason. A lot of people have hurt me. Though they were all family. You're not related, so I think we're good."

"Family," I agree with one word and a roll of the eye that indicates my disdain for such structures.

"Is your family local? You're from Direford?"

"Well, I don't know who my dad is. I think he was a soldier. My mum drank herself into an early grave when I was sixteen. So. Yes. I'm local. And classy."

A reply that blunt usually makes people uncomfortable. Nina nods. "I lost my parents a long time ago, and then my brother twice, sort of."

"To lose a brother once might be considered misfortune. To lose him twice seems careless."

She stares at me for a long moment, then covers her mouth and lets out a laugh.

"We should take the car and go into Direford," I suggest.

"Bryn wouldn't like that."

"Well, who really gives a toss what Bryn likes. He doesn't own you. You're his wife. About time you started acting like it. Giving him shit. Letting him know who is boss."

"He is my boss," she smiles, patiently. "Just like Thor is boss of you."

"Thor's not fit to be boss of my little toe, I'll tell you that much..." I would finish the sentence, but Thor's big hand just descended onto my shoulder.

"You set me up!" I laugh. "Nice. I'm going to fucking ruin you, but well played."

Nina gets up, smiling and gives me a saucy little wave.

"What was that?" Thor asks for clarification with his clipped, accented tone.

"I was telling Nina you're not my boss."

"You're right," he says. "I'm your owner."

I start to laugh, but then I realize he is really not joking.

"You're an absolute maniac," I say. "Truly, seriously demented."

I am so torn. Mrs Crocombe's food is amazing, and as long as I'm here at the abbey I seem to be able to keep the awfulness of what I did yesterday at bay. Nothing feels real here. I think that's why I tolerated the dungeon cell. After everything I've been through, the bath with Thor, the punishments, the interrogation, the bacon, it just felt right to curl up beneath a scratchy blanket in the depths of the abbey with a butler standing vigil and fall asleep.

But, of course, I'm going to escape.

"Bryn and I need to discuss what's to be done with you," Thor says. "There are crimes to answer for."

"I haven't already answered for them?"

"You think a couple of little spankings are atonement for arson, theft, and murder?"

"Well, not when you say it that way."

"You're mine," he says, his hand clasping the back of my neck. "And I'm not going to let any real harm come to you. But, Anita, you are going to be very sore, and very sorry before we are done."

He's threatening me. I don't know what effect he thinks that will have. It excites me, and it makes me more determined than ever to demonstrate to him just how little control he has over me.

"You stay here," he says. "Mrs Crocombe will keep an eye on you. Bryn and I are going to work out how to clean up the mess you've made. You can help by not making it any worse."

"Bryn's down there shirtless," I tell him, pointing to the door at the back of the kitchen that Bryn disappeared into. "If you were wondering. Maybe you should take your shirt off too. So you match."

He cuts his eyes at me, letting out a little growl of fury. I think I am tempting him. There was real desire between us yesterday in the bathroom. He is a lustful creature, I imagine, when he is not trying to desperately control that which cannot be controlled. But instead of taking his shirt off, he walks away. What a pity.

10

Anita

Mrs Crocombe is a lovely cook, and no jailer. I thank her for breakfast and go on my way. At first, I plan simply to walk back to the village, but as I am leaving the building — without any kind of interference from anybody, may I add, these are strange priests indeed who assume I might keep myself a prisoner here — I notice that the car is parked out front.

I also happen to notice that the keys remain in the ignition. There's only two types of people who do that: rich wankers, or people who need a quick getaway. They're the former. I am the latter.

I consider for a second that this might be some kind of trap. Or a test. Regardless, it's an opportunity I am not going to miss. I want to go into Direford, get my shit before Stephanie throws it all out, and see what's happening in town. I am feeling guilty and curious in equal measure.

I slide into the driver's seat and run my hands over the steering wheel. They could come out now and stop me if they wanted. But they don't seem to want to. I've become that strange kind of invisible again, where people aren't paying the attention they should. It seems to be my destiny.

The car purrs to life as I turn the key. I wait for people to come out. They don't. I suppose the cellar where Thor and Bryn are having their shirtless discussions is soundproof.

"Well. I suppose I am leaving."

And I leave.

It's a nice car. Fast. Manual. I don't often drive manual. It makes some very unhealthy noises on the way down the hill into the valley. And some really interesting smells. Burning rubber, mostly.

∽

I pull up outside my place. Nobody is in. That's good. I want to get in and out. I'll leave a note for Stephanie and what's left of my food and cushions for Brad. I just want my clothes. I can't wear Nina's castoffs forever. I want to feel comfortable in the jeans I've worn into submission, and express myself with shirts that curse at people when they read them. Simple things bring me pleasure.

Fortunately, I don't have much. Everything I own can fit in my rucksack and my duffel bag. My entire room packs down in about twenty minutes. Clothes don't take long to pack when you just hurl them into your bag.

I'm on my way out when Stephanie meets me coming up the stairs. She stops dead and looks at me like she's seen a ghost.

"Anita! Where have you been?"

"Just out. Why? I've come to get my things, by the way. I'm going to be moving out. You can rent to someone who has money to pay rent."

"The police were here. They were asking after you. Someone was killed in the village yesterday."

"That's unfortunate."

"They asked me to call them if I saw you."

"I'll drop in at the station," I say, shouldering my rucksack and my duffel a little tighter. This isn't good. There's no reason for anybody to look for me, aside from the fact that I'm guilty. Obviously, I don't want the police to think I am guilty. "Did they say what I could help them with?"

"Someone saw you running through the rain covered in blood. It's all over Direford."

"Shit."

We stare at each other.

"You're not going to... me, are you?" She's terrified. After all these months of flatting with her, there's finally some respect in her tone, and it's only because I'm being accused of something heinous without context.

"No, Stephanie. It wasn't me, obviously. I'll go clear it up."

I walk past her. She flattens herself against the stair wall to keep as far away from me as possible. I could get used to this kind of treatment. But I'm not going to. The last thing I want is to be arrested.

Tossing my possessions in the back seat, I get into the front and make a getaway. A real getaway, because I am sure Stephanie is already calling the police. She won't be able to help herself. She'll want the positive feedback. Stephanie's dream is to marry a judge, but I think she'd sleep with a constable.

I should get back to the abbey before anybody notices that I've taken the car. It's possible I'll get away with this completely.

But before I do go back, I just want to do a quick swing by Craig's place. It's not the brightest idea I have ever had, but my curiosity is stronger than I can resist.

As I approach at a reasonable speed, there's a bit of yellow tape out the front gate, and a small collection of officers wearing plastic suits over their clothes. They're swarming the place at a slow and painstaking pace. I can see them holding little plastic bags of what I guess must be evidence.

My DNA is going to be all over his house. And my fingerprints. I touched so many things. I briefly wonder if they have my prints on file, and then I remember that time I got caught shoplifting. They took my prints then. I am going to be positively ID'd six ways from Sunday.

And then things get worse. One of the officers meets my gaze as I crawl by. She's a thin-lipped, eagle-eyed sort with straw-blonde hair sticking out under her cap. I look at her. She looks at me. Then she looks down at her phone, where I am guessing there's a picture of me. Then she looks back at me and gets on the radio.

At this point, I lift my middle finger in a salute. Why, I don't fucking know. In for a penny, in for a pound. I'm no longer at a sensible thirty miles per hour. I'm hitting a *get the hell out of here* sixty before I know what I'm doing. This is a car that responds to the will of its driver like no vehicle I have ever encountered before. I put my foot down, it roars like a beast and leaps forward.

Unfortunately for me, apparently a murder in Direford has brought in police from across the region. They come out of the side streets like it's a movie, three cars swinging out of our little village lanes to assemble behind me, lights and sirens going. Direford has not seen excitement like this in forever.

I am not worried. When you have this much adrenaline coursing through you, you're not worried. You're wired. I know I can lose them in the countryside. There are roads, lanes, and tracks webbing all over this green and pleasant land. I just need to make enough turns at enough speed.

Screeechhhhhh!

That's the sound of tires, brakes, and bodywork all screaming at the same time.

It's been a while since I drove any car, and though this is one of the nicest beasts I've ever been in, I'm not the best driver. The stone-walled country lanes come at me fast, scraping the sides of the vehicle and curbing the tires. Shit. I'm going to fucking kill myself.

The cops haven't lost me. There's a real chance I'll crash before I lose them. I have to focus. I have to...

"God help me!"

I've never called for divine intervention before. I don't know why I'm doing it now. I know I'm in danger of the mortal kind. Every corner is another opportunity for disaster, and stopping is not an option.

"If I might be of assistance, miss."

Crichton sits up in the back seat, and I scream in shock. Where the fuck did he come from?

He leans between the seats, perfectly composed, not a mousy brown hair out of place.

"If you'd like to move over…"

"I can't! They're chasing me!"

"Slide over the center console. I'll take the wheel."

He's so calm I find myself doing what he tells me to do. I dive for the passenger seat, abandoning the wheel and expecting us both to end up in the prominent ditch. But that's not what happens. Suddenly, he's in the driver's seat. I didn't see him get into it, but he must have slid through that center console like a snake.

He has the wheel and we stop sliding around and hitting bits of road. We straighten up, and the car is suddenly one with the path ahead of it. The police are still behind us, but Crichton is in control.

Thor

Bryn is glowering at me intensely. I am attempting to regather the Brotherhood, but that is proving difficult. I hold a finger up, asking him silently to wait. I have one of the other brothers on the phone, someone capable of dealing with the matter at hand. Anita is the least of our worries. The blood trade happening in Direford beneath our very noses is much more of a concern.

"I'm not coming back there," Cosmos insists. "Bryn summons demons at his convenience. He lives in a house of demons. We are demon *slayers*. I can't abide being expected to follow someone who breaks every rule we have at his slightest convenience."

Cosmos looks like a rebel but talks like an authoritarian. Blue hair, tattoos, and piercings can't make up for a soul destined to make rules and ruthlessly enforce them.

"We are sworn to protect the blood at all costs. Besides, things aren't crazy like they used to be. I swear. He's married. He's settled down. Nina has had a calming and moderating effect. But there is blood trade happening, and we need to keep it out of the hands of the true enemy. I have reason to believe our old friend Craig was supplying Fleish directly."

"Fuck off," Cosmos curses.

"You don't need to come here, but I would appreciate you gathering those whose anger is not too great and going to Germany. A targeted raid on any Fleish laboratories is warranted."

"That's something you'd usually lead. You delegating that to me?"

"I can't leave the abbey at this time. There are other matters to attend to."

"You don't trust Bryn on his own," Cosmos says. "You know he's a fucking maniac."

"It's really not about Bryn," I say. "Let me know if you want to undertake the mission. If not, I'll come and lead it myself. Talk to you later."

I disconnect the call.

"I can go to Germany," Bryn says. "I trust you'll look after Nina in my absence."

"You can, and perhaps you'll have to. But it's time Cosmos led a mission. He's more than ready. His anger at you is something we can use to our advantage. A schism in the Brotherhood doesn't have to mean we are inefficient."

"What would we do without you, Thor," Bryn says. His sarcasm is at a lower level than normal. Close to heartfelt.

"How can I help you?"

"It's about Anita."

"She's with Crocombe."

"Yes. Well. I don't want her with Nina. Ideally, I don't want Nina and Anita crossing paths at all. Nina is an angel. Whatever Anita is, it isn't going to be good for her. She's far from the companion I would have chosen for Nina."

"You know that sometimes you talk about Nina as if…"

"As if what? She needs guidance?"

He knows what I mean. I don't have to outright say it. Nina is so young. And so innocent. And Bryn, bless his soul, is older in so many ways. Even his eternal spirit bears marks of advanced age and suffering. He wants to protect her, and yet he cannot. Not from life itself.

"You don't guide her, Bryn. That implies that you let her experience the world. She stays in this house, day in, day out. She barely walks the grounds. Someone like Anita would be good for her. She needs female companionship."

"Not that kind of female companionship. She needs someone well read, well educated, and..."

"That's an excellent point. Are you going to allow her an education? She hasn't attended university. Or will she grow old in this house without ever experiencing the world?"

"I didn't come here to talk about Nina!" Bryn is beginning to lose his temper. "I came here to tell you to keep your little delinquent away from my angel."

Little delinquent is a generous description of Anita, I suppose. Maybe he is right. She's older than Nina, and that means she risks becoming a role model. Anita is in her mid-twenties. I need to verify her age. The problem with becoming soul-bound to another hammer wielder via the medium of murder is that one skips a great deal of the getting-to-know-you phase.

What I do know is that Anita is old enough to have passed through the idealistic phase and lost enough hope to become dangerous. There are a lot of people around her age wandering this and other counties becoming increasingly dangerous. Their anger is righteous, for the most part. But she is my responsibility. Anyway, my thoughts have diverged.

"I can keep Anita away from Nina," I say. "Assuming they do not seek each other out, which is a real possibility. Your wife is lonely, Bryn, and fate has seen fit to bring us this woman. Anita is here for a reason, in the same way all things happen for a reason. She's part of the Lord's plan."

"We both know he makes some spectacularly shitty plans," Bryn snorts. "Let's keep them apart for now. Until you have Anita tamed."

"We spend far too much time worrying about these girls. We have a local murder investigation to worry about. The police could come looking for Anita at any time."

"Would that be the worst thing?" Bryn is unsympathetic. "She deserves prison."

"We both know she'd never have killed anyone if we weren't trying to sell peeks at the hammer for fifty pence a go."

"Right. The roof. I forgot about the roof. Such a tedious imposition."

I think he is referring to the roof and not Anita. None of us are domestically inclined. That is what the service demons are for. Well, theoretically, when they are not doing the bidding of cursed objects. The ongoing crumbling of the Brotherhood has cost us in so many ways. Once upon a time we would have had the craftsmen to complete the repairs ourselves. Now we are at the mercy of the mundane labor market.

Bryn and I look at one another with a similarly morose expression. We would both rather do battle with a demon army than deal with these tedious matters.

"Where is Crichton? He's usually fairly good at handling these affairs."

"I haven't seen him the last hour or two," Bryn says.

"He abetted Anita with the hammer. Have you noticed that both he and Crocombe are particularly enamored of her? They're not usually interested in humans of any kind. Even compared to Nina, they show a strong preference for Anita."

"Yes, the girl you've managed to bind to you in blood is more popular than my wife," Bryn growls.

"That's not what I'm saying. I'm..."

I do not get to say what I am saying because Mrs Crocombe has appeared in the doorway, wiping her red soapy hands on the dishcloth tucked into her waist.

"Fathers," Mrs Crocombe says. "I've just heard word from Crichton. Seems the young lady has taken the parish car and is now being chased through the dales by the police."

"How is that possible?" Bryn looks aghast. I probably do too.

"She's reckless, impulsive, and opportunistic. That's how it's possible," I growl.

"If you come up to the roof, you can see..."

I find myself clearing steps three or four at a time to the roof. Crocombe was right. We can clearly see the black outline of the parish car being driven at high speed through country lanes.

Anita has an uncanny ability to make me feel helpless as she forces me to watch her behave in outlandish and outrageous ways, holding herself and our bond at high-speed hostage. Does she know she matters? How could could she? She barely knows me at all. I am a stranger to her. First, I was a mark, then I became a monster.

I want to thrash her. And I will. But I have to forge some kind of bond with her, or this rebellion will be endless — until it comes to a tragic and entirely foreseeable conclusion.

A*nita*

I've never seen the countryside coming at me this fast. Crichton handles the car like a rally driver, and I finally feel safe enough for my brain to start working again.

"Were you in the back of the car the whole time?"

"That would appear to be a reasonable explanation for my presence now," he replies, glancing in the rear-view mirror. It's not really necessary. The sirens are still very much audible. These country police have never been so excited to catch anybody. Direford isn't a place boasting a lot of high-octane crime.

I wonder what Crichton is going to do to get us out of this. I am a passenger now, and that gives me time to do what I so rarely have opportunity to do. Think.

"You weren't in the back of the car. I put my duffel in there."

He doesn't reply. But I know very well that men cannot appear from nowhere. The whole thing about being a person very much involves being one place, and then being in another. Things that don't have to be anywhere in particular before being somewhere else are not of this world.

"You came to me last night with the hot chip butty," I say. "It was so nice, and this is nice too. So I don't want to throw any of this in your face. But..."

The butty was delicious. Mrs Crocombe must have put it together in the middle of the night just for me. I can only imagine her having a fry up in the wee hours of the morning, then sending Crichton down to me. The two of them have been so very kind to me. They are they only ones who've seemed pleased I was there. Bryn and Thor would rather I didn't exist at all. Yes, even Thor, whose desire has been evident from time to time, and who has shown me some softness, he'd probably wish he'd never met me.

The tires are squealing and the car is sliding from side to side, but Crichton keeps it on the increasingly narrow lanes with the ease of a rally driver.

"Why are you on my side?"

"Because you're one of us, miss. You knew what was in the case the moment you saw it. Unlike the generally dull public, you were drawn to power, because it comes from the same place you do."

"I really don't know what you're talking about."

He smiles gently and navigates the car around a sharp bend, over a hillock, and through a portal to Hell.

Literally.

Before I know what is happening, the hill in front of us is no longer a gentle rise with a calm track ascending. It is jagged rock, a hole torn straight through the earth and reality itself. I didn't see it open up, surely such a tectonic event would destroy everything for miles around. But there's not even a shudder. There's just the strangeness and the openness, and a cavern made for two before us. The road fractures into a thousand pieces, but Crichton does not slow for even a moment. He presses his foot even closer to the floor, going faster, accelerating into the maw of the world.

"Don't tell anybody," he winks. "The Fathers get ever so cross when we do things like this."

I am too busy being shocked by my sudden new surroundings. Instead of England's green and pleasant land rolling by the windows, there's a lake of fire and presumably brimstone on either side and great red rising hills upon which ancient buildings stand. I can see figures moving around in the distance with slow and shambling gaits that speak to pain.

"Are we in Hell?" I cannot believe I am asking that question.

"Oh, yes. You can see the fresh souls simmering in the lake. See their hands?"

I thought the lake was filled with strange rivulets, but actually it is covered in the tips of waving fingers of those who have been cast into it by winged demons who catch them as they come falling through the roof of this world, and then toss them into the lake directly.

It is a horrific and terrible sight, and yet I cannot take my eyes off it, because it's also the coolest fucking thing I've ever seen, all this demonic power on display at a moment's notice.

"Cool."

"Not cool. Very warm. Positively boiling. You know, those who take the lives of others spend much longer in the lake than others."

"I thought everybody spent eternity there."

"Oh no. Hell is much more than a lake district. There are many ways to punish a soul which has strayed."

I can't stop staring. I know I am supposed to be horrified. I am horrified. This is all terrible. But it's also awesome, in the old testament meaning thereof. I am awed.

The journey ends too soon. Before I know it, there is a gleaming portal to the world above, ringed in gold. The road goes up and through that portal. Crichton drives us up and out of Hell and when we emerge, we are in the courtyard of Direview Abbey, safely behind the walls encircling the rear, and well out of view of any patrolling policemen.

"I suggest you prepare yourself," Crichton says. "Your punishment is next to come, and I imagine it is arriving on swift wings."

No sooner has he warned me than Thor bursts out of the abbey's rear door. I never noticed the ornate carvings on that when I was first taken here. It catches the afternoon sun, and I can't help but see that there is a skull among the roses and thorns.

Less than a second later, my entire view is Thor. He's massive. And ripped. Literally. The shirt he's wearing has given into the force of his musculature and popped open along the length of his shirt, displaying his chest and a lot of his abdomen. Maybe he was only half-dressed when he heard us pull up like a near literal bat out of Hell.

"What the hell were you thinking!?"

It is just as well I never put my seatbelt on, because he grabs me out of the car so roughly, I am sure bits of me would be left behind if I'd been restrained.

"You steal a car, go back to the crime scene, lead the police on a chase and get yourself on a most wanted list? You are never leaving this property again. You are grounded, for the next decade, at least. You..."

I tune out at that point in the threat parade. There's no point listening, it would only stress me out, and I have plenty to stress me out already. Today has been wild. Maybe even wilder than yesterday, and yesterday was one of the wildest days I could conceive of.

"Anita!" Thor gives me a shake. "Are you listening to me?"

"I saw Hell."

"What do you mean? You're in a hell of a lot of trouble..."

"I mean we drove through Hell. Like down through the ground, into Hell, and back up again. Toot toot!"

He keeps hold of me but swivels toward the butler.

"Crichton..."

"Her statement is factually accurate."

Thor lets out a roar of rage. Real fury emerges from him, reaches the sky, and calls forth a great plume of rain. We are instantly soaked, but he does not seem to notice the rain.

"This madness ends here and now." He holds me aloft to face him. His features, always handsome and strong, are still twisted with that anger which makes my stomach churn to behold. "I cannot lose you. You are the first in over a thousand years to hold the hammer and to have it act through you. You are special. You mean something. And you are determined to throw your life away as quickly as possible."

He has tried so hard to convince me he is just a normal man. But today I saw Hell and now I am seeing his true face. The face not of a man, but of a god.

"I... it wasn't intentional," I tell him. "The chase, I mean. I just wanted my clothes and things. I sneaked down to get them so I wouldn't have to keep wearing the trackies."

"And you ended up most wanted. Do you know what this means?"

"Yes. It means they want me for murder. Which is fair, because..."

Rain turns to hail and I rethink my impertinence. Whoever I am talking to... whatever I am talking to, he's more powerful than I've ever given him credit for. I've mistaken his mask for his true self. Most people's masks are more impressive than the reality behind them. He is the exact opposite.

Crichton has disappeared. I don't blame him for making himself scarce.

I am coming to a series of swift realizations that were before me all along. I ignored them because they did not fit with the reality I have been uncomfortably nested in my entire life. I knew the hammer was special the moment I saw it. I knew what it was, even. But I didn't believe myself. Even as I was taking it, using it, feeling its power course through me in a dark electric bolt...

"You are a god."

"I am not," Thor growls. "But you are a little demon, and I know how to handle demons. They must be punished."

"Fine by me."

"Fine by you!?" He lets out a roar of laughter that causes clouds to cluster above, ripe with dark anticipation.

"You're THOR! You can do what you like to me."

"You're right on one count. I can do what I like to you."

The electricity is not limited to the sky. It is zipping through me, from my head to my toes, and mostly to my core. I've been through some shit today. I've seen more than any living person I've ever heard of. I've been through Hell. Now I'm hoping this angry Viking will show me heaven.

You'd think I'd be worried about something else. One of the many existential revelations, perhaps. The confirmation of the literal existence of Hell, for example. But I'm just fucking horny.

The adrenaline, the rage, the power, the danger.

He drags me indoors, up to his room. He continues to snarl like a vicious thing. No words emerge from him whatsoever. He's just making noises I cannot translate into any kind of language, except the language of sex and revenge.

My clothing is ripped from me. Nina's Juicy suit is destroyed in the hands of wrathful god. I am thrown onto the bed. He is not being careful with me. He is barely treating me like a human with human limitations. He is treating me like a thing to be punished, someone who deserves to be hurt. And yet he's not hurting me.

He holds my legs apart, splaying me lewdly. In the fuss and furor of his lust, his own clothing has suffered the same fate as mine. He is magnificent. He is broad shouldered and he is powerfully muscled. I am not a small woman, but he makes me feel diminutive in his presence. I am beneath him, in every sense. I am waiting to be claimed, because that is what I am in his eyes, a thing to be conquered. A soul to be owned.

I don't fight him because I don't want to. I've wanted this from the first moment we met. I think this was inevitable somehow.

He is inside me, thrusting deep, spreading me wide. His thunder god cock makes every bit of me spark. I give myself up to him completely, knowing he is angry with me. Furious, actually. this isn't a hate fuck. It is a fury fuck. My pussy is being roughly punished by a literal god and I know I deserve every stretching, aching stroke.

"You belong to me," he snarls, his hand clasping my jaw, keeping my eyes on him. His cock is as deep inside me as it can go, stretching me to my very limit. I can feel my pussy clenching him with desperate need, trying to milk his seed into my cunt. I'm such a filthy little slut when it comes to him.

"Do you understand? You physically belong to me. I own you. You no longer exist for yourself. You breathe for me."

His possessiveness is more intense than anything I have ever encountered. I am more than wanted. More than desired. This doesn't end when he's finished. This goes beyond the length of his dick. I am claimed. I am his.

My orgasm rushes through me with the force of a tidal wave, rushing though my every nerve and thought. I feel like I'm being erased in some fundamental way, every bit of me that's not screwed to my fucking soul is gone.

⁕

I feel like I need a cigarette, but I don't smoke. The sex was just that intense, the kind of mating that makes a girl ache in all the best ways.

"I can't believe I fucked the ancient god of…"

Thor sighs. "I'm not the ancient god."

"You're going to keep telling me that after everything I've seen?"

"I'm not. Let me explain, as best I can. It will be overly simple because it is too complex to explain in detail. I'm not *the* Thor. But I carry a part of him inside me. A shard of the divine is lodged in me. If it is ever removed, I will pass away instantly. I am alive by his grace, standing guardian over his tool. I am the only one who can handle it or understand its power.'

"Well, I don't have any shards and it worked for me, so maybe it's been upgraded?"

He gives me a flinty look.

"We are talking about the sacred weapon of a power beyond understanding, not the latest smartphone. I do not know why the hammer chose to work for you. It may be that you have some qualities yet to be discovered. A human taken to Hell is not allowed to simply leave. The fact that you were allowed free passage both in and out is as concerning as it is astonishing. I know who you are. But I do not know what you are."

I don't know what I am, either, but I don't mind. He might think I have some special talent or hidden secret, but I know better. I am as average as they come. I am just in the presence of someone extraordinary, and that makes me extraordinary too.

"It's like a riddle. What can use the hammer of the old gods and pass through Hell unharmed? Me!"

"What can turn a temporary immortal gray? Also you," he groans. "Anita. You must not be so reckless. I can cage you, but inevitably you will have to be free. When you are, I have to be able to trust you not to do anything so mad you require a demon to save you."

"I can't promise anything. Because I don't want to be a liar. I don't know what I'm going to do half the time before I do it."

"You need to develop self-control."

"Probably. Easier said than done."

"I'll help you. You just need discipline."

I need more than discipline. I don't think he understands how impulsive I am, and how impossible those impulses are for me to control. I stole his hammer on a whim.

Now I'm wondering if I'm not just a very good little puppet who dances on the strings that make us all jump about very well. I don't fight anything. I do what makes sense at the time. Sometimes not even what makes sense. Sometimes I just do what I'm doing.

"I don't think discipline is going to work. That's the thing about me, Thor. I don't care what's going to happen later. I never have. It's like consequences don't exist until they happen and by that time it's too late. I'm not trying to be a fucking prick. It just happens."

"Thank you for being honest," he says. "You are what we are. We're all what we are." As he speaks, he's wrapping silken ties around my wrists. I'm tired, but I reckon I can go another round, especially if all I have to do is lie there and let the demigod or whatever the hell he is thunder inside me.

But he doesn't tie me up to fuck me. He ties me to the bed, one arm at each corner. He then proceeds to do the same to my ankles until I am naked, dripping, spread-eagled, his captive. He tosses a light blanket over me then stands there, hands on his hips, looking generally satisfied.

"You're going to be bound, restrained, and even caged when I can't watch you," he tells me. "That's the only way I will ever know you're truly safe. I have someone else I need to deal with."

T*hor*
"Crichton!"

If it is possible for a demon to look hang dog, he does. Crichton has served Bryn's family for longer than any of us have been in existence. I've not chastised him before. What right did I have then? Now I have every right.

"If you wish to lecture me, sir, know that I have already been thoroughly rebuked by the master. He has made it most clear that guests to the house are not to be taken through Hell itself."

"I have tied her up in the bedroom."

"Very good, sir."

"Do not let her out. Under any circumstances. I don't care what she says. I don't care what the hammer wills. She, and it, must stay in their respective places. Am I understood?

"Yes, sir. Absolutely, sir."

I need to speak with Bryn. This situation has reached a head and cannot continue. Something has to give. Something has to happen. I just don't know what.

I find Bryn in his library, reading. He's not usually a reader, and I doubt he is taking in any of the information in the book. I think he's sitting there, stewing on recent events. He was not happy to have Anita here in the first place, and he's almost certainly less happy now.

"I think she's a psychopath."

"Probably," Bryn says, barely looking up from his book.

"No. I mean really. She doesn't connect cause to effect. She's pure chaos because she simply doesn't care about consequences."

"You sound excited about that."

I do sound excited about that, but I know I shouldn't be. "The hammer responds to her. She was allowed passage through Hell..." My thoughts are coming more quickly than I can express them. They're not strung together in a coherent order. They're just there, circling my mind, attempting to make sense of themselves.

"She's a demon," Bryn says.

"Yes. I mean. No. She's not, or obviously you'd have been overcome with the desire to slay her. She's not a demon. But there's a little demon in her. Or a little deity."

"We are all blessed in various ways," he says, turning the page.

I am more than a little affronted that he is not listening.

"Am I boring you with the revelation that we may have a new spark of heaven or hell in our midst?"

Bryn looks up from his book, dark eyes cool. "A little," he admits. "She's your problem, Thor. I have a wife to worry about. And a roof to fix. And the Brotherhood is being forced to deal with Fleish on their own, which is a significant concern, given we appear have allowed blood trade out of our bloody parish. Forgive me if I am not fascinated by the provenance of your latest conquest."

"She's more than a conquest. She's blood bound to me."

"Yes. And she's still a terrible influence on Nina."

Selfish prick. Bryn cannot see further than the end of his own nose. His wife. His abbey. His failures. He is not a popular figure among our number, and he seems disinclined to do anything to amend that.

"Perhaps I should take her back to Norway with me. Get her out of your hair."

"Maybe," Bryn says. He's looking back at his book.

This coldness is not like him. He is usually all brimstone and fury. To see him sitting there pretending he cares about words printed on a page is concerning.

"What is wrong?"

He slams the book shut. "We are losing control. We are losing power. We are becoming irrelevant, and all you can do is fuck a local."

"A local who can wield the hammer of Thor."

"Anybody can use a hammer. She's a filthy slattern, a waste of breath, and she's... standing behind you."

I turn to see Anita standing behind me, just as Bryn said. She looks very upset. She has reason to be, after the tirade he just unleashed concerning her.

So much for tying her up. Why did I trust Crichton to guard her? He has been on her side from the moment they met. There's something very strange going on, and in this moment, very socially awkward. Anita unleashes on Bryn with predictable fury.

"Do tell me how you really feel. A filthy slattern? You cradle-robbing dirty old man! Keeping that poor American girl locked up here like some kind of fuck toy. Ought to be ashamed of yourself."

"Anita!" I snap her name.

"No. Fuck him."

Bryn takes out his phone.

"What are you doing?"

"I am telling the police where she is."

"No. You're not. Don't be ridiculous."

"What's so ridiculous about turning in a wanted criminal who has committed arson and murder in the last week? You're not thinking straight, Thor. You're blinded by lust. I've seen it happen before, and I will not see it happen again. We protect the bloodlines. We do not provide sanctuary for murderous locals. Hey! Give that back!"

Crichton has materialized just in time to snatch the phone out of Bryn's hand. A full-bore mutiny is taking place now, and Bryn is not well pleased.

"It would not be proper to turn her into the human authorities," Crichton says. "I believe there is some essence of demon in her..."

"I am bound to slay demons, Crichton. Something you might want to remember," Bryn threatens.

"Very well," I say, before matters can get out of hand even more than they already have. "I will take Anita home with me. She is mine to take care of. We'll vacate the premises, as so many others have done before us. Your temper and your inability to accommodate the needs of others is doing damage to the Brotherhood, and to you, Bryn."

11

Anita

Apparently, I'm a little demonic. That's not surprising. It's not even a current topic of conversation. The argument between Thor and Bryn was verbal, but brutal. I'm sure they both said things they're going to regret, but they're both still too angry to regret them yet.

I'm sitting on Thor's bed, watching him pack his suitcases. He has two. One big, one smaller. Everything goes into them perfectly folded. The chests and wardrobes are being divested of their contents. He's working methodically and quietly. Strange, for him. I'm used to him raging at me.

"How are you so calm?"

"I'm not calm."

"He called me a slattern."

"He did, but don't take it personally. He doesn't know you. And he is not angry at you. He's furious at himself. It's not easy bearing all the conflicting responsibilities we must bear."

"Like what?"

"For one, we protect those who have angel blood. It is very rare."

"And it's Nina. Isn't it. He's obsessed with keeping her pure."

"Yes. And then, on the other side of the equation, there is Fleish. The man you called Craig was in league with them. They are traders of blood, occult cultists. A group of lost souls who believe that they have the flesh of Christ."

"What do you mean the flesh? You mean the body?"

"Yes."

"The literal body"

"Yes."

"The whole body? Like a mummy?"

"On that, they're not entirely specific. But if they have even a sliver of flesh, or a piece of hair, it is possible that they will achieve their goal."

"Which is?"

"They are trying to unite the blood of angels with the flesh of Christ to genetically engineer the apocalypse," he sighs, as if it is a minor annoyance.

"Sounds mental."

"It's utterly mad. But it's also possible that it will one day work. Never underestimate the power of someone with a mad enough idea and the motivation to make it happen."

It sounds like good advice.

"So where are we going, exactly?"

"I am taking you somewhere far from everybody and everything. I need to make you mine so completely you can never again get yourself into this much trouble."

"How am I going to get out of the country? I'm wanted. And I don't have a passport. I doubt they issue passports to people who are wanted."

"A private plane."

"You've got a private plane? You didn't have a thousand pounds for your hammer, but you have a private plane?"

"It's not my plane. It belongs to a friend."

"Should have asked the friend."

"Friend may be the wrong word."

Speaking of friendship... "I feel bad I made you and your friend fight."

"Bryn is Bryn. Have no fear, we are as strong allies as ever. Direview is rarely occupied by the Brotherhood, though it is our home. We are difficult men, and our personalities rarely mesh. Of all the things you can comfortably be blamed for, this is not one of them."

I find myself admiring Thor. I've pushed him to the limits of his patience and perhaps even sanity, and now we're running off because Bryn has basically banished him over me, but he doesn't hold grudges. At all. That's not to say he's warm and snuggly. He is as dictatorial and dominant as ever, but he's not angry. His rage does not control him.

I could run away now or try some other way of getting out of his possession, but I don't think I want to. I want to stay with him. I want to see what happens next, in Norway. It's curiosity that keeps me by his side as he packs us out of the house.

Nina waves from one of the upper windows, a pale American ghost held captive by her brooding husband. I feel sorry for her as I wave back.

"It's not right, you know."

"What's not right?"

"Nina and Bryn."

"You know nothing about them, or their relationship. Worry about yourself. Believe me, there is plenty for you to worry about."

∾

The private airfield is not all that far from the abbey. Crichton drives us there. There are no detours through nether realms today. Disappointing. I'd hoped he'd give me another little sneak peek of eternal damnation, but he's remaining firmly on the mortal plane. I don't want to go anywhere without him. He's become like a security blanket for me, a magical, demonic entity who makes everything all better just for me.

"Hey, Crichton. Any chance of you coming with us?"

He shakes his head and appears mournful within the bounds of his own limited emotional range. "I'm afraid not, miss. I am bound to Direview and its immediate surrounds."

"Well, if I don't see you again, give my love to Crocombe and have my thanks for saving me. If it wasn't for you, I'd be in some real trouble right now."

"I would not make the mistake of assuming that because you have avoided prison, you are not in real trouble," Crichton says.

When Thor says things like that, they sound like threats. When Crichton says them, his words sound like a warning from a concerned friend.

"Time to be on your way, I think," Thor says, dismissing him.

I don't think Thor approves of the alliance between Crichton and me. He's angry about the trip to Hell thing, I'm sure. But he didn't want me being apprehended either, so Crichton did us both a favor, but Thor's not open-minded enough to consider that. He wants control of the situation, and that means stripping away anybody who might be allied to me. From first we met, he has been trying to keep me from associations of power. I suppose I was trying to steal his hammer at the time, but still. One could call it a pattern.

"Bye, Crichton. See you soon, I hope!" I wave.

Crichton gives me a slight incline of his head, which I know stands in stead of a more emotive farewell. I'll miss him. I don't know him as well as I might, but I know he was on my side. There haven't been that many people in my life who have helped when I needed them to. He's on a very short list, so even the fact that he's a demon who drove me to Hell doesn't dull my affection for him.

He purrs away in the parish car and I am left with Thor standing in front of a hangar on a rather uninspiring grass airstrip. If he tries to put me in some rickety tin can of an aircraft, he is going to have some trouble. Flying is unnatural, and if I'm going to do it, it's not going to be in some smuggler's coke transport.

Thor puts his hands to one side of the hangar and draws the door back. Corrugated iron slides away to reveal the prettiest plane I've ever seen. Prettier than any plane I have ever imagined, even. It is jet black with gold embellishments along the wings, wings painted over wings. Like a great big metal bird crouched and ready to take to the skies. It's stunning. Like a piece of art.

I turn to Thor, who does not seem to be as moved by it as I am. I guess he is used to it. What a dark horse he is. So much of him remains completely unknown to me. So much of everything, apparently. I am surrounded by surprise, and it is making me feel more alive than ever before. The last few years of my life have been nothing but eking out a basic existence, trying to somehow make my limited resources stretch to both support myself and make my life worthwhile.

Now, on the heels of some of the worst things I've ever done, I'm having the time of my fucking life. I have had sex with this man, this absolute fucking god, whether he admits it or not, and it was amazing. I don't even care that he's probably technically kidnapping me now, because my will doesn't matter at all.

"You have been holding out on me," I tell him. "This is not a plane owned by a man who doesn't have a thousand pounds for an artifact."

"I haven't held out on anything. I told you, I don't own these things."

"You just have it sitting here at your disposal."

"My patron is generous, put it that way."

"Your patron? Who is your patron? Fucking Midas himself?"

The closer I get, the more the details stand out on the plane. Someone has gone to the trouble to paint every single feather of the pretend wings atop the plane's wings. This is art only the sky will see, and I suppose the people who clean the plane. And fly in it. It's designed to impress, and it is working.

I don't know what the word for whoever owns this plane is. Magnate? Oligarch? This has to be one of the most expensive things I've ever encountered. Direford's not a rich place. I've been to London, of course, but the wealth there is different. It's expected. And it's surrounded by average, ordinary things that taint it. This plane is a pristine piece of beauty just waiting to be exploited. There is a blonde lady in a pilot's uniform standing by the open door ramp. She's not smiling, but smiling is becoming an increasingly rare expression these days in my immediate vicinity. Besides, I'm British. I'd be immediately suspicious as to what she was up to if she smiled.

"And you had a pilot on standby? Or is the pilot a demon too?"

"Stop asking questions and get on the plane." Thor nudges me. He's very much not in a good mood. It's a pity.

"You should relax and try to enjoy yourself," I tell him. "Life's too short."

"Yours is poised to be especially short if you're not careful," he growls at me, grasping the back of my jumper and propelling me up the stairs. "Let's go. Now."

At the top of the stairs, the plane is revealed to be as luxurious as one might imagine.

"I feel spoiled," I say, sitting down in a leather armchair.

"You are spoiled," Thor growls. "I should probably put you in the baggage hold."

"And even that's probably nicer than anything at Direview. That place is a rotting dump."

He gives me a warning look to let me know I am testing his patience, then takes the seat opposite me. In this setting, he's suddenly elegant. Massive, ancient, but also refined. I'm still not entirely convinced he's not actual Thor, though I suppose actual Thor has better things to do than slum it in Direford with a slattern like me.

"Does this flight come with champagne?"

"It will come with intense pain if you don't stop enjoying this quite so much," he growls at me. "This is no holiday. This is what I must to do tame you. I need to take you to the source of the hammer's power and see how you resonate. Now. Put your seat belt on."

12

Anita

The flight to Norway was unfortunately brief. Less than four hours later, we are descending. I always thought I'd be a bad flier but being in this plane has made me convinced I might be a very good flier. It's like being in a much larger car. There are some lumps and bumps but flying through human skies is far smoother than taking the little-known laneway to Hell.

"So where are we going?"

"To my home," he says.

I feel as though his accent has thickened merely from being in Norwegian airspace.

"And what's your house? A castle? Is it also owned by your patron?"

"You will see soon enough. I would appreciate you attempting to behave yourself, if you can possibly manage that."

"I will see what I can do."

He sighs and propels me down the stairs from the plane. This time he keeps a hold of my jacket to keep me from falling. What a gentleman. I notice he keeps his hand there even after I am safely down. Maybe it's not so much about helping me after all.

"So this is Norway?"

"Yes."

I am used to gray, green drizzly places. This is a much more intense version of England's landscape. The green is deeper. The grays are darker. The sky hangs with heavy menace, and the rocks themselves are larger and older. Everything is -er er.

We've landed much as we took off, at a private airstrip. The terrain here is much rougher and rockier, not quite mountainous, but absolutely in the realm of foothills. There's a mountain up behind us, and not far from the airstrip, there is a carriage waiting, hitched to two heavyset pale horses with black stripes running down the center of white manes.

"Cool ponies!"

"Norwegian fjord horses," Thor says. "Floki and Odvar."

"They're your ponies!" I gasp with excitement. I never imagined I'd be sleeping with someone who had horses. These two look very sweet. I continue to be absolutely thrilled by all these turns of events. "And I get a carriage ride!"

. . .

T*hor*

She has been taken from England in disgrace. I will grant that the methods of transport thus far used have not exactly helped to impart that feeling, and her glee at the horses and the destination is charming. I wish I could forget all she has done and simply enjoy the way she is reacting, taking pleasure in her happiness. But I cannot.

"Get in the carriage."

She scowls at me. She is so beautiful when her temper rises. She's truly exquisite. And she's entirely mine.

"You don't have to be a tosser," she says. "You're ruining Norway."

"Ruining Norway," I laugh. I can't help it. Perhaps I don't want to help it. She is right. I am ruining this. And not just for her. For me too. Bryn wouldn't like what's going on here. He'd want her punished and tamed. He'd want her absolutely ruined.

But she doesn't belong to Bryn. She belongs to me. And seeing her standing here in the wild Norse air, with her curls flying about her head and her eyes gleaming with native mischief, she makes sense. She has found an immediate context. Who am I to take it from her, to crush her spirit and thrash the life from her?

"I'd like to show you my home," I say. "Please. In the carriage."

Her expression softens slightly, following mine.

"You know," she says. "You really don't have to loathe me. I'm sorry I stole your hammer, but subsequent events have made it fairly clear that was destined. Did I really even have a choice? As for getting chased by the constabulary, yes, I grant you, not an ideal series of events, but again... there's a fatedness to all of this, don't you see?"

"Are you trying to tell me that every time you criminally misbehave it is actually fate's fault?"

"Yes!" She snaps her fingers and points at me. "Got it in fucking one."

"Get in the carriage, Anita."

She does as she is told, grinning with amusement at her own impudence.

I allow myself a smile when she cannot see me. I don't want to encourage her. She needs a firm hand and a hard limit. She needs to know where the boundaries are, or she will commit atrocities, of that I have no doubt.

Fortunately, the sense of wonder she seems to be experiencing is doing wonders for her behavior.

"Fucking hell! Look at that!"

We round a corner, and she loses her composure well and truly.

A*nita*

"This is my church," Thor says.

"This is fucking..."

Describing this building would stretch the abilities of the most able bard. I am not an able bard. I am a slattern from

Direford. *Slattern.* That insult is going to stay with me for quite some time.

It looks like an old church decided to wear a lot of other old churches as hats. There are a lot of roofs over it, triangular constructions hanging heavy over other triangular constructions. Each of those roofs looks like it has been finished with wood dragon scales. There are four gables, presumably aligned with the four most popular directions, and every single one of the tips of those is adorned with a carved dragon head.

"Cool."

I finish my sentence with a word that doesn't capture it at all. This is so much more than cool. It is awe-inspiring. It touches some part of me I didn't know was there. I feel reverence in a way I never have. I feel connection. I feel like I could stand here and stare at this building all day and all night long, watching the world turn against the unruly skies.

"It is cool," Thor agrees, his lips twisting with the understatement. "The trees from which this place was built no longer grow where mortal men may access them."

"But immortal men might be able to?"

"Everything is eternal in its own way. This world is temporary. What is in it, is not."

"Very philosophical," I comment. Thor's a lot more intellectual than I've given him credit for while being distracted by his glorious flowing hair and massive muscles. To be fair, much of our conversation has been centered around how terrible I am and how generally awful I behave and please would I stop blackmailing him for his prized possessions.

"So you're actually a priest?"

"I'm ordained, yes. And I have responsibility for this place, yes."

"A Norse god becomes a Christian priest?"

"Not a god, and sure, why not. It's all much of a muchness; these human definitions of the divine mean very little in the end. We are all ants attempting to describe the same elephant."

"Except your elephant has a hammer that calls thunder from the skies."

"Life is not as simple as we would have it be," he repeats. "I hope now we are away from the scene of your many crimes, barring any new crimes, we should be able to discuss the deeper nature of what is happening."

"You mean I might get some answers."

He looks at me with intensity. "We both might."

"Tell me how you ended up with a god shard inside you." I go right for the first and most obvious answer. He keeps claiming to not be actual Thor, but there is something undeniably divine about him.

"It wasn't an easy or pleasant experience. I will tell you, but first I would like to go home and get warm." He shivers. "This air is flowing straight from Niflheim."

There is a bite to the wind, but I am a well-insulated person and I'm just so thrilled by my new surroundings I barely notice the cold.

"Where is your house, then?"

"Up over the hill. You cannot see it from here, but from there you can see all over the valley."

"Like Direview Abbey."

"This place is even older than Direview."

He says that with some pride. I gather that there must be some cachet in having a particularly old and impressive place to live among these so-called brothers.

"Who else is there? Do you have house demons, like Bryn?"

"I would not be caught calling her a house demon," Thor says. "My mother lives there."

"Aw, that's sweet. You look after your old mum."

"My mother would not be pleased to hear you describe her as old."

"Oh, so she's a cool, young mum? A milf?"

Thor's expression is one of pure horror at the term *milf*. I cannot help cracking up. What a lark this all is.

"You should have warned me you were taking me home to mummy dearest," I tell him. "I'm not exactly mum safe."

"Try to be polite. Or at least sane," he says. "She's seen more than you can imagine, and she knows everything you want to know. She could be your greatest ally. Or, if you choose to make an enemy of her, she'll be useless to you."

"So you're saying I should be on my best behavior and try to make a good impression."

"Can you do that?"

"No. Not really."

He sighs and palms his face. "You are such a brat. There are not enough thrashings in the universe for you."

The carriage rocks on its suspension as he drags me over his lap in a last-ditch effort to make me compliant.

"Oh yeah, spank me!"

I feel him hesitate and can't hide a smile. He's so easily manipulated. If he thinks I like being thrashed, he's liable to stop it.

"You're... impossible," he growls. "How am I supposed to get a grip on you when you absolutely refuse to be..."

"Gripped?" I fill in his words hopefully.

His palm descends on my ass in a solid smack.

"Fuck, yes!"

He spanks me harder. Hard enough to make it impossible to pretend to be unaffected by it.

"Fuck!" I curse one word, and I mean it. My ass is suddenly blazing with heat and aching intensely. Thor repeats that same stroke again and again, making his bloody point with my pain.

"You're going to be respectful, obedient, and lawful. And if you're not, you can expect to experience pain like this a thousand times over. Direview belongs to the Brotherhood. This place belongs to my family, and you will not sully it by being a..."

"Slattern?"

"Brat," he finishes, slapping me so hard I cannot offer another word. All I can offer is a cry of pain as the carriage turns and begins to ascend at a quicker pace. The horses like to go faster uphill, for some reason. I guess they like making things harder for themselves, or maybe its the driver making them work harder. I didn't catch sight of them before. I wonder who it is. A demon? No. I doubt it. The world can't be full of helpful demons turning up at useful interludes. I do miss Crichton already. Funny how you can get attached to someone who saves your life.

I am much more out on a limb now. I am at Thor's mercy. And he has never been interested in mercy. I think I have gotten lucky, in a manner of speaking, because I have given him so much trouble. He can't keep up with all the insane events he's had to respond to. But there's a silence out here, a quietness among these barren lands that concerns me. This is a place where people get their comeuppances.

He finally stops spanking when we arrive. My first view of the house is one from a low angle, and with an ache that will stay with me for some time. It is impressive. Of course it is. There is nothing about this man that does not impress.

Thor's Norwegian home is stunning but heavy and imposing in the same way Direview was. It's like the Norwegian cousin to the abbey. There is a spire and a tower, not to mention multiple high, gabled walls. Much like Direview, it is oversized and unnecessary unless one has a small army, which I am willing to bet Thor does not.

It strikes me suddenly, though it should have struck me before. It didn't, though, because Direview is such a run down, semi-abandoned, demon-infested mess of a ruin that I never really thought of the inhabitants as being rich. But the private plane and the carriage and the mansion cannot be ignored.

"You are fucking loaded. You could have wired home for money when I took your hammer. You could have paid me ten thousand pounds without it mattering at all. You could have stopped me from becoming a murderer."

"I could have done a lot of things. I did what I did."

He's completely unrepentant. I still hardly know Thor. Our relationship mostly revolves around theft and revenge, and I guess now we're adding being outcast to the mix. I wonder if he's annoyed at having to leave Direview with me, or if it is a relief.

One thing I am starting to become aware of is the privilege he comes from. He was playing poor in Direview, but it's now apparent he comes from money and power, two things I have never had.

We alight from the carriage together and approach the house. Thor keeps my hand in his. He's keeping me under control in as limited way as possible. He doesn't want it to look like he's worried about me. His big hand over mine is a substitute for a collar and leash around my neck.

We're almost at the ornate door when it creaks open as if by its own will.

"You did not send word of your coming, Thor." A woman's voice emanates from the interior. "We have not had time to prepare for guests."

"I am not bringing guests. I am bringing my things."

Sassy. And hardly an appropriate way to introduce me to his mother. She's probably going to be shocked and appalled.

We're not going in, I notice. We're just standing here, waiting for something. Permission? An invitation? Who knows. After another long moment or two, a figure emerges from the shadows within. Thor makes his introductions dutifully. I can't help but notice that there is no filial joy here. Not a close family, not in the traditional way.

"Anita, this is my mother. Skathi, this is Anita."

Skathi is tall and thin and icy, from her frost-colored hair to her flinty eyes. She is clad in a dark dress with lace accents, understated, but menacing. When looking at this woman, I see the end of all things. I shake the feeling off. Making snap judgements about a person is wrong, especially if you think they are literally the end of the world.

"Hello," I say. "I'm Anita. I'm from England. I killed a man with a hammer."

Skathi looks over my head at her son. "This is the woman you bring home? This hearth has seen nothing but ash for years, and now an English woman with no verbal filter enters our sacred space?"

"I am invading you lot," I joke. "Turning the tables. You know. Like, the Viking thing?" I make general Viking sounds and motions, which are harder and vaguer than one might imagine. There is a part of me that knows I am making a fucking idiot of myself. There is another part that finds that funny. And then there's another part that is curling up in a ball and hiding from mortification.

"I'm going to take her upstairs," Thor says apologetically. "She's tired. She's not usually this..."

"I am usually this, though," I say. "I'm usually worse. I haven't called anybody a cunt yet. Oh, there I go."

"What are you doing?" Thor growls in my ear.

"I'm not going to make a good impression, so what's the point in trying?"

He drags me upstairs. At first, I can't make out my surroundings. This house is kept in the dark. The curtains are drawn. The great windows are pretty from the outside, but they do nothing for the inhabitants. Skathi clearly cares not for light.

By the time I am bundled into a room, my eyes have started to adjust. That just means they are shocked once more when Thor throws the curtains open and casts the whole room in light.

It is sparsely furnished. I do not have much chance to observe the finer points of my surroundings, because Thor has me by the shoulders and is filling my vision.

"Really, Anita. You can't hold your tongue for one moment? Not even two minutes of polite behavior?"

"Your mum doesn't seem happy to see us."

"She doesn't like being visited on short notice."

"Sure, she was busy sitting in the dark and then we show up and get in the way of all that..."

"You don't know what you're talking about. As usual. You speak before you think. You speak before you *see*."

"Your mum hates me." I saw the distaste in her expression. I heard it in her voice. Thor's wrong when he says I don't see or think. I do both faster than he realizes. I knew within seconds that my presence here was not welcome and might not even be tolerated.

"No. My mother knows whoever joins me in partnership will have a painful and difficult life."

"Oh, excellent. Really selling this here, you know."

"I don't need to sell this to you. You're already caught up in it so tightly you couldn't escape if you wanted to. I'm trying to explain the dynamics here so you find it slightly easier to exist."

There's a knock at the door.

"Skathi would like to invite you down to dinner, sir." A disembodied voice comes through the door. A house demon, no doubt, or perhaps a human sycophant with no need for sunlight.

"Clean up. Wash your hands. Brush your hair."

He's worried about what I look like. He wants to make a good impression. Sweet, but futile. Has he already forgotten why we are here? I am in exile.

"Can't brush curly hair. Makes it look mental. You don't need me looking crazy on top of everything else."

"Then come downstairs and try not to make everything worse."

"I will try."

∽

"What was your profession before you became a murderer?" Skathi is attempting to make polite conversation in a dining room lit by candles. The curtains are drawn against the cold day. I wonder if she's sensitive to the sun. There are some people who are allergic to ultra violet radiation. She could be one of them.

Thor looks at me. I could try being polite too, I suppose. Let me try.

"Oh, I didn't have one. I just sort of scraped by. You know begged, borrowed, lived cheaply. Wait. No. *Sustainably*. That's what it's called now when you have fuck all. I was incredibly sustainable."

Skathi shoots Thor a look. She must be horrified. I am sure she always imagined her son with someone more appropriate. A valkyrie, or a Nordic model.

"This is really good food, by the way. Thank you."

I'm not lying. It's fucking delicious. Mutton and cabbage don't sound good to a lot of people, but when you've lived most of your recent life on a diet of perished perishables, real meat and vegetables are luxuries. Crocombe's food was very good too, but there's something extra special about the fare a mother prepares for her child. I know this isn't for me. She made it for Thor.

"I'm glad you're enjoying your meal," she says. "Does your mother like to cook?"

"My mother is dead. So her cooking's been limited."

"I'm sorry to hear that. And your father?"

"God knows. Or maybe he doesn't. I definitely don't know."

"Ah," she says, as if I make sense now. Poor little orphan Anita. Her pity makes me bristle, though I know it is well intended. I'd rather be disliked than pitied, if I'm to be honest.

"I know. Your god son has dragged a stray in. But guess what? I used his hammer. It worked with me. Through me. And that means I am not utter rubbish. Even if I used to eat out of the rubbish. There's a lot of nutrition in bins."

Skathi looks shocked again.

"Anita..." Thorn warns me.

"She's trying to get to know me. I'm helping her. I'm not going to lie to your mother. Is that what you'd like me to do? Lie to her?"

"No. Of course not. But the details don't need to be quite so... detailed."

I return to eating and spare everybody my attempts at conversation. I know I don't belong here. I know I don't belong with Thor, really. I'm an accident.

Eventually the food is gone and then I am sent back up to the room. Thor takes me and locks me in with the iron frame bed and the little wooden bedside tables. This room should be full of fine things. Instead it is furnished with the bare minimum. It's not his room, then. It's just a room we have been assigned together. I wonder if he asked for us to be assigned to this place of spare parts where nothing truly belongs.

"I'm going to speak to my mother. You should get some rest."

"Thor?"

"Yes?"

"I don't belong here."

He hesitates a moment before leaving. "Nobody does."

T*hor*

She needs time to settle. I need time to think. I did not imagine I would find myself exiled back to the remote Norwegian wilds with a little murderess. First she took my hammer, then she took my life.

My mother is waiting for me outside. The sun has set, and she still enjoys her evening strolls. I accompany her and together we walk the grounds. We stroll in silence at first. We have never been conversationalists, she and I.

"You like her, don't you."

"I love her," Skathi says, the skin about her eyes crinkling with the warmth she has been hiding.

"I was afraid of that."

"You shouldn't have told her that I am your mother. It's an untruth she'll discover. She's here for the truth. Give it to her."

"You gave me life. That makes you a mother. That's truth enough for now."

"Thor, if you keep deceiving her, it will end in more than tears. It will end in pain. Yours, and hers. You brought her here, to me, because you knew I would not allow deception."

"I brought her here because the moment she put her hands on my hammer, she was out of control, and I don't think she can be brought back under control. Not in civilized society. There's something about her, Skathi. Something unnatural. I don't understand why the hammer responds to her. Is she one of yours? Is she demon spawn?"

"One of mine? She might have been, once. Now of course, she's just another person in a big wide world of oh-so-many people. Being special is no longer special."

"You don't understand, Skathi. She's not merely a little wild. She's absolutely out of control."

"Then control her, Thor. By any means necessary. You were going to do that anyway. That's why you brought her here. Why do you pretend to hesitate? Are you looking for my blessing?"

"I'm looking for your help, for an explanation…"

"But you already know the answer, child," she says patiently.

We have circled the house and returned to the front door.

"It is time to go in," Skathi says. "Time to deal with the one you love."

"THOR!"

I hear Anita screaming my name, almost as if on cue. Things happen with a strange sense of timeliness here. The fates are strong. Everything happens for a reason and a meaning.

Her cry of fear and perhaps pain is enough to send me flying up the stairs, three at a time. I burst into the room and find her sitting up in bed, soaked in sweat. She must have fallen asleep, but that sleep was clearly not restful.

"What's wrong?"

"I dreamed about..." She takes a deep breath. "The hammer, and what I did with it to that man."

"I'm sorry." I wrap her in my arms and snug her close. This is the first time I have witnessed anything like a conscience in this woman, and it is very reassuring to see. I was beginning to think she was a stone-cold psychopath incapable of regret and therefore incapable of other softer feelings, like love. This breakdown, painful as it may be, shows that she has potential.

"I cracked him open like a fucking Kinder Egg," she sobs. "And then he was just... everywhere. All over me. And he was..." She shudders in my arms. "Warm. That's what body temperature means, you know?"

"I do know."

"And it was on me. Sticking to me. In my hair..."

"I know. I washed it from you."

"You did." She looks up at me. "You were there for me. In the grossest way possible. I mean, truly disgusting."

"Yes," I agree. I cannot hold back from smiling. There is ever a sense of humor about her, a lightness even in the darkest moments. I used to think that lightness was part of her pathology, a sign she didn't feel the darkness. But that's not true. It is her way of desperately trying to claw away from it.

"I want to see all the things you consider disgusting," I tell her. "Not just the brains of your fallen enemies, but the other things you hide away inside. The feelings. The fears."

She lets out a groan that might almost be a growl. "It's easier not to."

"I know, and yet, I'm going to make you. Because if you don't, you're going to be as much of a monster in your waking hours and tormented by them in your dreams."

Anita

All this talk of sharing feelings and truths, and he's still a complete mystery. Seems hypocritical, and I intend to point that out.

"You still haven't told me what happened to you. What made you what you are, what gave you the hammer, what..."

It's his turn to screw his face up. He doesn't want to relive whatever it is. I feel bad for making him, but he is the one insisting on talking, and he is the bigger mystery.

"If I tell you, it is something you must keep between us, and it is something you must not question. I have told nobody what happened to me all those years ago, because it is stranger than anybody will believe."

"I'll believe," I promise.

"I died," he says. "My family and I all died. It was an accident. We were skating on an icy pond near the home, one that had been skated on for generations. And one day, for a reason we'll never know, the ice cracked. Every single one of us went in..." He pauses and takes a ragged breath, like a boy trying to suck air into his lungs. "My father was not a strong man, not a well man. He wasn't able to save us, and the waterlogged winter clothes dragged us all down. Me, my sisters, my mother, my father. All the way down to the bottom. I was seven years old, and I remember it. The cracking of the ice, the water so cold I almost didn't feel it. When something is that cold, you become part of it faster than you know."

"You seem very alive," I point out.

"Skathi took me from the ice. Unlike me, she is a goddess. Literally. She lifted me from the water and she placed a shard of the hammer inside me. Yes, it is a relic of great power. You already knew that. It has the power of death, but it also contains the power of life. It animated me. It made me alive again. And it gave me power. Made me a tool of the god. So the hammer is mine, insomuch as it is me. As in, I am it. You didn't steal my hammer. You stole a part of me."

"Fuck," I curse. "No wonder you were so angry. And no wonder you had it just out and about. Didn't think anybody would go running off with your leg or soul."

"Quite. I should have been more careful."

I cuddle up to him, grateful for his honesty. I understand him so much better now. I know why I felt drawn to his pain, even though he seemed strong and rich. There is a part of him that will forever be wounded, eternally trapped at that age of seven, drowning and dying in the cold waters of this land. I feel a deep sadness for him. For the first time, he doesn't feel like an adversary. He feels like someone I might truly love.

Then another thought occurs to me.

"So I told a goddess, a literal living goddess, that I eat rubbish."

"Yes. You did."

"Why did you say she was your mother, you prick!?"

"Because she rebirthed me, gave me new life. I owe her my existence."

"And what did she want in return?"

"She needed someone here, to navigate the modern world, to mediate between her and these feral moderns, and to do the work of the gods."

"To join the Brotherhood, you mean. That still doesn't make sense. They're monotheists. And don't start talking about elephants."

"How about I don't talk about elephants. How about you talk about you."

"There's nothing to tell. My dad was a one-night stand, probably. My mum was a drinker, and I've looked after myself for as long as I can remember. I steal, I scavenge, and I lie. I stopped going to school at fourteen, but I've always liked reading so I know more than I should, but I've got no qualifications, and I don't want any."

"So you saw the hammer and you had to have it."

"Maybe, seeing as it is you, I saw you and just had to have you. Maybe this isn't about gods and murders. Maybe it's about soulmates and love?"

I smile broadly. I'm almost teasing. But I guess there's some part of me hoping for a midnight declaration of love and devotion. It is possible that all this opening up is leading to the great love of my life.

And then it doesn't.

He doesn't smile. He frowns.

"But the hammer should not respond to you the way it does. It shouldn't work for you. It…"

Still going on about the fucking hammer, right in the middle of our romance. It feels like rejection. It *is* rejection.

"Are you mad the hammer responds to me the way it does, or are you concerned that you react to me the way you do? It's like you never had a choice. I saw you. I wanted you. And I took you. It's not supposed to be like that, is it? The man is supposed to do the chasing and the wanting and the claiming. You didn't even like me."

"That's not…"

"This is what talking about feelings is like, Thor. It leads to hurt feelings. You can go now. I can have nightmares on my own."

I feel so ashamed. I thought we were about to have a truly tender moment. I thought he was going to tell me he wanted me. But that's not what he's saying. He's rejecting me. His confusion is a pointless way to keep me at arm's length.

"Anita…"

"Go away. And take your stupid hammer soul with you. Don't worry. There's nobody here to murder. Just you and a goddess."

"Anita..."

"GO. AWAY! I don't like you anymore. I don't want you. I don't need you."

I am so embarrassed, I let myself be suckered into this feelings talk with this absolute dolt of a god-possessed Norwegian who doesn't even like me. I killed with his dumb hammer, and now I am stuck with him, and he's stuck with me.

"Go to whatever room is yours, the room you didn't want me in, and leave me the fuck alone."

He gets up, and he does what I've asked him to. I watch him leave and wish I was back at Direview. Wish I was in Crocombe's kitchen, or Crichton's company. They knew how to comfort me. How to care for me. Thor is just as cold as his icy goddess of a mother.

Sleep evades me. I am upset. More than upset. I feel absolutely hopeless, on the verge of wanting to just give up. Why is it so wrong to want to be wanted? I don't know if I even want him to want me anymore. I think it might be too late for that.

Looking out the window, I see the night unfolded all around the house. It's calling to me, offering to envelop me. It might be the only embrace I get. Pathetic, sad, and small as I feel in the aftermath of comfort turned cold, I decide to go out.

∼

I am not alone.

"Skathi?" I say the woman's name, knowing that she is not a woman. I am in the presence of the cold and the divine. I am also fairly certain I am butchering the ever loving hell out of it.

"Anita," she says, a faint spell curling the corners of her lips.

"Thor told me about you," I say, somewhat awkwardly.

"Indeed."

"So. Uh. What is it like?"

"What is what like, child?"

"Being a goddess?"

Her eyes brighten a little in the moonlight. "You are an uneducated little thing, even your own secrets remain hidden to you."

Well, that seems like a rude response. Maybe goddesses lack social graces because the rest of us are beneath them. Maybe talking to me is like talking to a worm. I think I would be more polite to a worm, though.

"What are you mulling?"

"If I would be nice to a worm."

"Seems like you might know what being a goddess is like after all," she smiles.

"But you're here, all alone in this house. It seems boring. If I were a goddess, I would be out doing cool goddess things. I'd probably try to rule over something."

"I am sure you would," she says patiently.

"Do you love Thor?"

"Like a son."

"Me too. Not like a son. But I love him."

"How nice for you."

I am shivering. I wrapped myself in a coat I found at the front door as I went out. I think it might be Thor's. It smells like him.

"What do you do?"

She looks down at me from her great height, and for a moment I see her not as a woman, but as a tree, stretching from the Earth to the Heavens above. She's more like a node of connection than a person, a being of great, ancient power. She branches. She creaks. There are a few places where her ice cold bark drips with rich sap. She is wounded. She is perfect. She is eternal.

Asking her what she does is like asking what the sky does. She does not need to do. She just needs to be.

"Woah!"

"Indeed," she says.

"I suppose my concerns seem petty to you."

"They are transient, but important. You have been brought to a place of great power, Anita. There are forces all around you, confluences of fate and intention that will wrap themselves around you and use you like a puppet if you are not careful. You should listen to Thor, and worry less about love. It will not serve you here. This is not a place for romance. It is a place for the dead."

I stare at her, and as I stare, her pretty face begins to wither away until I am looking into the dark holes of a skull. I scream, but the wind takes it away. I am alone. I am lost. I am facing my end...

***

I open my eyes to morning. I am in the bed Thor left me in. Alone. That was a very powerful dream, though I am not convinced it was a dream at all.

I get up, put yesterday's clothes on, and go downstairs in the hopes I'll find Thor. I end up following my nose, which is directed by my stomach to find food. At the end of a hot, buttery trail of scent, I find everything I am looking for.

"Sleep well?"

He asks the question while sitting behind a stack of toast the likes of which only people in eating contests have ever seen.

"Yep. You?"

"Fine," he says.

I take some toast and butter it in the heavy silence that inevitably follows a tiff. He's not talking. I'm not talking. We're just aggressively chewing. Sakthi isn't here, which is probably good seeing as she's a goddess ghost tree who haunts my nightmares and warns of doom. That would be a bit much over breakfast.

"Coffee?" He offers.

"Please," I accept.

We may be in Norway, but this is all very British and incredibly awkward.

"I do not know what to do with you," he announces at length. "You seem to have no natural conscience at all. This is a place of last resort. If I cannot tame you here, there will be nowhere you can be controlled."

"Maybe you should worry less about controlling me."

"I'd love to, but history has shown you cannot be trusted."

"What am I going to do here?"

"I don't know," he says. "That's what I am afraid of."

"Morning!"

We both startle as a blue haired man with a reckless grin walks in wearing boxer shorts and a vest with a dragon on it. He looks like he's just rolled out of bed. He's obviously very much at home. Maybe another one of Skathi's children?

"Cosmos. What are you doing here?"

Cosmos, apparently that's his name, yawns. "I came to see Skathi for some career advice."

"You're supposed to be dealing with Fleisch."

"Who says I haven't?"

"So you've conquered the trade in angel blood?"

Cosmos drops into an open seat next to me and winks, ignoring Thor's question entirely. Unlike Thor, who occupies vast amounts of space with his breadth and presence, Cosmos is leaner, but I'd wager no less powerful or dangerous. There's something mysterious about him. "Hello," he says. "You must the one driving Thor mad. Nice to meet you."

"I'm Anita," I smile. I like this guy instantly. He's got a way about him. A dark sort of ease. Thor, and Bryn both have a kind of authoritarian bent. This brother seems much more chaotic. I like that.

"How have you heard about Anita?" Thor is curious.

"There's whispers among the brotherhood that someone lost his hammer to a girl," Cosmos smirks. "Rumor travels fast."

"Does it? I know it doesn't come from Bryn. You don't talk to him."

"Crichton lets the brothers know what they need to know."

"I will be having words with Crichton," Thor growls.

"Embarrassed you got shown up by a local girl? Is that it?"

"Are you a priest too, then?" I interject with a question to save Thor from having to rip Cosmos' head off.

"No," Cosmos laughs.

"He was defrocked." Thor seems pleased to offer that information.

"Defrocked," I snort.

Cosmos' eyes flash blue amusement. "It's not as much fun as it sounds. No. I'm pretty much outlaw everywhere."

"Hey, me too! High five!"

We clap hands overhead while Thor looks on with a dour and increasingly concerned expression. I think he's finally understanding what Bryn meant about the bad influences in the home, thing.

"Cosmos is a murder and a villainous wretch currently shirking his duties to the Brotherhood," Thor growls. "Do not make the mistake of being charmed by him. That is a veneer that can be scratched with a thumbnail to reveal a complete monster."

"You do know you're selling me to your girl, right?" Cosmos says.

"Don't worry. I'm a one god kind of girl," I assure Thor. I'm not interested in Cosmos, but I imagine a lot of women are. There's something about a handsome, devil may care, reckless rake of a stranger that makes the blood rise with the potential for terrible decisions.

Thor grunts, and that sound reminds me all over again that I'm not actually his girl. He's not embraced me the way I want him to. He's keeping me at arm's length as a sort of hammer related curiosity, good enough to fuck, not good enough to commit to.

"Wow. Temperature dropped in here," Cosmos notes. The tension is thick enough to cut with a knife.

"I'm going to get changed," I say, making my excuse to get the hell out of Thor's presence.

T*hor*

"So what are you doing with that one?" Cosmos flicks his eyes toward the door Anita just went through. "You going to marry her? Have babies?"

"She's wanted for murder."

He shrugs, like I knew he would. Cosmos is the walking definition of having no standards whatsoever. "*I'm* wanted for murder."

"I don't want to marry you and have your babies either," I tell him.

"Ouch!"

My feelings are complicated. Obviously I am devoted to Anita. I have no choice - and it is that lack of choice that makes me worry in turn that what is between us might not be fated so much as it might be a curse.

"You overthink everything," Cosmos tells me. "And that's what makes you fuck things up. You try to be careful, and you end up fucking things. The girl likes you. Don't waste it."

"I don't think you're the person to give me relationship advice," I tell him. "When was the last time a woman didn't run from you screaming?"

He laughs, teeth flashing with amusement. Cosmos is hard to rattle. The world rolls off him. It doesn't matter how many times he commits unspeakable atrocities, kills someone, commits a heinous crime, or just behaves lawlessly, he always seems to get away with it.

"I'm not a relationship sort of guy," he says. "You, on the other hand, are. Imagine how sweet you'd be with a wife and a family."

I keep my own counsel, though the truth is such things feel as foreign to me as they do to him. I am not made the way most mortals are. I tried to explain that to Anita, though I doubt I succeeded. I am never going to be a father. What animates me is not like what animates other men. If she is to be with me, she will have to sacrifice all the goodness a mortal marriage could give her. It is not just that she is asking me for my heart. It is that in giving it to her, I risk taking everything from her.

A selfish bastard like Cosmos would never understand any of this. His idea of being with a woman is ravaging her to a breathless orgasm and leaving before she recovers. His partners are always willing, and equally transient.

"Hello, my boys."

Skathi enters the dining room with her usual elegance and presence. Cosmos waves and bites into some toast. I take her to task.

"You could have told me he was home."

"I have the same entitlement to be here as you do."

"You're not even Norwegian!"

"So?"

"Don't squabble. There is enough room for the both of you here," Skathi says patiently. Cosmos and I are something like brothers while also being absolutely nothing like brothers. He is not endowed with any special god shard. He is a maniac. He appeals to her appreciation for the chaotic, much like Anita does.

Sometimes I feel as though I am the only responsible one left on the planet. The only one who thinks about his actions, the only one capable of enforcing rules, and reason.

. . .

Anita

I'm the odd one out again. The one who doesn't belong. I don't know how I've managed to spend an entire life being unwelcome and out of place, but here we are.

I've gone outside. The mansion is too oppressive. It feels more like a labyrinth from which I might never escape if I get too comfortable. I wonder how many unwanted lovers are in there. More than one, I imagine. I do not think we are the only guests, and certainly not the only residents. Skathi's home is large enough to house a small army, and I've seen no real evidence to suggest it doesn't. They're just all introverted and late to breakfast, probably.

The snow has melted somewhat. I see dull grass and bits of rock peering out all over the place in a fairly dismal sort of way. I do find myself wondering if this is a real place. It feels real, but I'm also almost certain that somebody normal setting out from Oslo in a rental car could never reach here.

I am distracted by such esoteric thoughts by the sight of horses. The Norweigian horses truly are built completely differently from the standard English nag. They're short and tough and powerful. They're all grazing rough grass. As I approach, they lift their heads and prick their ears at me, interested.

The closer I get, the closer they decide to get.

"Hello, ponies," I say.

They sniff around me to see if I have any treats. I don't have any, and they quickly lose interest and go back to eating. I like the horses, they're peaceful to be around. They're not offended by my presence, or indifferent to it.

"Anita!"

Thor comes striding across the pasture. "I didn't know where you were," he growls, as if that is an issue I need to worry about. "Don't wander off here, it's not safe."

"That'd save you the problem of trying to work out what to do with me."

That cheeky comment earns me a hard slap to my arse. Hard enough to bring me up to my toes and make me curse. Normal horses would run away at the cursing that explodes out of me, but the fjords barely move.

"I know exactly what to do with you," he declares. "Thrash you, bed you and hope for the best."

I'd like to say I won't sleep with him without a commitment, but that is a lie. Thor makes all the sense in the world out here. The cold Norse wind whips through his hair, making it blow magnificently. It also makes his shirt flag against his musculature. He's fitter than I can express.

"Come here," he says, taking my hand.

"Where are we going?"

"For a walk."

That's what we do. We walk together over whatever you call the Norwegian equivalent of moors. Every step takes us deeper into a desolate landscape that still feels somehow recursive, like we're walking toward a point on the horizon that isn't there.

"I died here, and I was born here," he says. "But I wish I did not have to bring you here. You should be back in the normal world, living your normal life."

"You think I'm normal?"

This might be the most offensive thing he's ever said to me, and I find practically everything he says to me offensive now. He truly thinks I should be slagging around Direford, begging for food and getting kicked out of my flat.

"I think you could be normal," he says. "And I think your association with me has taken that chance away. You could find a normal mate. You could have children…"

"Oh gross. Right. Go on the benefit and get a council house and pop out some babies for extra. That's what you think of me."

"I didn't say…"

"There's no perfect life waiting for me anywhere else," I tell him.

"So I am your last resort," he says.

"Oh for fuck's sake. Just piss off already!"

Another hard slap lands on my rear.

"Speak with respect. We have much to discuss, and I will not have you cursing at me every two minutes because I ask questions you don't want to answer."

"Smack me again, and I'll smack you."

He laughs at me.

His hammer is suddenly in my hand. I don't know how it got there. I don't know how I am able to command it, and right now I do not care. I swing that hammer. Not the same way I swung it at the angry German in Craig's flat, but in a sweeping motion that creates a massive arc of wind that hits Thor and sends him staggering dozens of feet away.

"Give that back!" He roars. He really hates it when I fist his hammer and refuse to let go.

"Come and get it!"

I hold the hammer aloft, and suddenly like Mary Poppins, I am airborne. Flying. Holy fuck! The power of this thing is truly awesome.

"Get down!"

Thor seems very small now, disappearing like a little ant. I am going up, up, a little too high for comfort. I lower the hammer and I start to go down again. Fast. Too fast.

"I'm fucking flying!" I'm now screaming toward Earth without any kind of ability to stop. The hammer has too much weight to orient it back up. I hold onto it with two hands, wondering if I am going to punch right through the Earth, or if I am about to be squished flat.

Thor takes a mighty leap up from the ground, reaches his massive fist for the hammer, and surges back up into the sky, drawing me back aloft like a plane pulling up at the last moment from a failed landing. He wraps his other arm around my waist to stop me from falling and looks into my eyes with pure fury.

He's saved my life. This does not seem to please him as much as it pleases me.

"Leave my hammer alone," he growls as he takes us safely back to Earth.

"It wasn't my fault. I don't even know where it came from!"

"You have to take responsibility for your actions, even if they're not your fault," he lectures, setting me back down.

"That makes no sense. I really didn't mean to almost kill myself just now. You have to believe that."

"You're trouble," he growls. "You'll always be trouble. I am not going to watch you die because you are reckless and irresponsible. And yet I can't seem to tame you."

As he speaks, he starts tearing my clothes from my body. I feel like a present being unwrapped, but by someone very angry and not at all thrilled to be receiving it. With a wild Norse god tearing at my clothing, I am very much entranced and enthralled. The adrenaline from my recent flight is still pounding through my veins, and now my heart beats for a whole new reason.

"What. Do I have to do. To make you behave?" He snarls the question in three parts, the last of which is punctuated by the tearing sound of my underwear being ripped off my body.

I've heard of hate fucks. This isn't hatred. This is something even harder to resolve. Thor grasps my chin in his big hand and turns my head up for a passionate kiss. He is still clothed, but he frees his cock, revealing a second hammer to try to pound some sense into me.

I am tossed down onto the mossy ground, mercifully avoiding the rocks. And then he is on top of me, his furred clothing making him look like the beast he seems to me to be. I see bright eyes peering viciously between narrowed lids as the wind whips his hair across his face and makes my nipples taut with excitement and yes, fear.

I know he won't hurt me. Everything Thor has ever done has been in service of saving me. But he is tiring of the game. His patience is wearing thin the same way everybody's patience inevitably wears thin where I am concerned. I know there has to be some part of him that wants to be rid of me. Instead he is going to go deep inside me. He lowers his head between my legs, holding onto my hips and setting about giving my poor pussy a tongue lashing the likes of which it has never seen before. I feel his hot, wet tongue licking at my sex, parting my lips, finding the dewy core of me. I think I must be cold, but I don't feel it. I feel hotter than ever, lit by some infernal flame that has always burned inside me. For long minutes he licks and he laps, and he makes my hips rise to his mouth with a grinding motion that speaks to how desperately I need him inside me.

And then, suddenly, his mouth is gone. It is replaced with the flat of his fingers, contacting my wet, swollen pussy with a hard slap that makes a yowl echo across the valleys and ridges of this rough and unforgiving landscape.

"Fucking ow!"

"Does it hurt?" He repeats the treatment again with an expression of satisfaction.

"Of course it fucking does!"

"Good."

I try to close my legs but he has no intention of allowing me to escape this particularly painful and intimate punishment. He pushes them back open with one hand and he sets about spanking my pussy with swift, harsh slaps that make me squirm and beg him for mercy we both know I do not deserve.

"Again, I am forced to watch you recklessly nearly kill yourself," he snarls. "Again, I am forced to wonder if these will be the last moments I have with you."

When he talks like this, it is as though he wants me, but when this passion is over and his fright settles, I know he will return to his questions and his rationalizations. I want to stay here with him, a bad girl needing punishment, his possession to be protected. I would rather have his anger than his confused indifference.

His spanking makes me sting and ache, the lips of my pussy growing red and even more swollen. At least two dozen strokes land against my increasingly wet cunt, my hips writhing, dancing a mold of my bottom into the moss below me. I start to moan almost as much as I gasp and cry out, because as always, Thor's pain is turning to my pleasure.

I could come like this. I could orgasm while he spanks my clit and my lips, punishes me like the bad girl I have always been, and always will be.

"Fucking hell," he curses, reaching up to clasp my throat. His voice is ragged, his breath harsh and growling. He wants control of me so badly, but I can't give it to him, no matter how much I try. My legs are already spread wide, offering him an obedient pussy sacrifice. He fists his cock in his other hand and drives it deep inside me in one powerful, claiming thrust. I feel myself stretched wide, my inner walls gripping him and struggling with the girth of his rod at the same time. Thor is big. Very big, and neither of his hammers can resist me. The literal and the metaphorical are both somehow bound to my flesh.

The sensitive skin of my lips and the hot bud of my clit rubs against his hard leather clad pubic bone as he starts pounding me. I have been spanked tender, almost to orgasm, and within a dozen strokes of his punishing cock entering me, I am coming. Hard. My cunt grips him with desperate need, trying to milk him. But he resists. He's not going to come yet. He's going to keep punishing me. Keep fucking me. Keep using me.

Thor

I shouldn't be fucking her. I should definitely not be letting her come this way, her entire body quivering and shaking around my dick. She is so beautiful, her body pale in the cold Norwegian light. In this place, everything is turned to ice. Everything is made frigid. But not her. She is the volcano in the midst of the icy plane of my existence. I cannot resist this woman, and that makes her dangerous to us both.

She screams with orgasm, flailing and arching, forcing her hips up against mine and taking me as deeply as she can inside that hot, furred slit. It is enough to almost tip me over the edge, but if I cannot control her, I can at least control myself.

I hold her beneath me and I slow my hips in the wake of her orgasm. I work my cock slowly in and out of her hot, red, glistening hole. What are the depths of this woman? Why is she so much more complicated than any other? Why is my attraction so intense? Her lips grip me on every stroke out, forgiving me for the punishment I inflicted on her and offering pleasure in its stead.

Her eyes are locked on mine. I can see an apology held in them, as if she is sorry for everything. But it is not an apology I can accept, because this is not over. This may never be over.

She reaches for my arm and wraps her smaller hands around my forearm as I thrust deep inside her. There is a fire inside this woman, an intense heat that bathes my cock and holds it tight and demands I give her what she wants. I have been determined to make her mine, but I think I might be hers. I think she might possess me in some inexorable and unspeakable way. I think I might be lost. And I think she might be where I can be found.

I fuck her hard. I listen to her whimper. I feel her submit. And I fill her with my seed.

A*nita*

"That was hot," I say when I get my breath back. Thor is holding onto my naked body as if he is afraid it is going to slip away.

"Please," he says. "Don't do anything else stupid."

"I didn't know it was stupid when I did it. That's the problem. You learn from the past. And I don't have a magical hammer past. I don't even know how it got in my hand."

"You summoned it."

"I think I might be magic too," I suggest.

"You're something," he agrees. He drops a sweet, affectionate kiss on the tip of my nose. This is a moment of rare softness between us. I feel a kind of acceptance I've not had before. I wish it could last, but I can already feel him slipping away in some intangible manner. I don't know what he's waiting for, or what he needs, but I don't think it is me.

"Does Skathi know? About me, I mean?"

"Skathi knows everything and says very little about any of it," Thor says. "You remain a mystery."

Those words are my doom.

He can't tame me because he doesn't understand me. That's not his fault. I don't understand me either. A heaviness is setting into my soul, a sort of inevitability that makes me start to accept what I cannot change. Thor and I are not going to be together. Not now. Not ever. It's like Skathi said. There's fate here, not fickle fortune. Something stronger, something inexorable that is pulling us apart no matter how hard we try to come together.

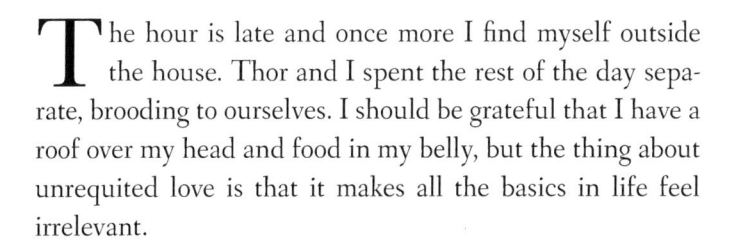

∼

The hour is late and once more I find myself outside the house. Thor and I spent the rest of the day separate, brooding to ourselves. I should be grateful that I have a roof over my head and food in my belly, but the thing about unrequited love is that it makes all the basics in life feel irrelevant.

The night is beautiful. From the house I can see not only the stars, but the church below. It is stunning. And wonderful. And a once in a lifetime view. Snow has fallen and covered the craggy ground, making the landscape pure and pristine. I am very fortunate to be seeing it. And I'm too pissed off to enjoy it. Because I think I might be heartbroken. I'm not sure.

Thor can't get past the fact his dumb hammer works for me. He doesn't see it as something that connects us in a good way. He sees it as some strange burden, and now I feel like I've forced myself on someone I never intended to.

Maybe I'm not pretty enough for him. That's it. He needs some willowy, elegant creature like Bryn's Nina. She's stunning. And I'm just a rubbish-eating local from Direford. He knows I'm rubbish too.

I know I should just leave, but I'm not entirely sure how I'd do that. I don't know how to harness horses to a carriage, and I can't fly a plane. There must be roads in and out of this place, but I have no money, and no passport, oh, and I'm fucking wanted.

This is not a good moment to realize that I've lost absolutely everything and yet, here it is. I have nothing. I don't even have someone who will feed me expired food anymore. I feel pathetic, and weak, and unwanted. I'd cry, but I'm afraid the tears would freeze against my cheeks and make me even more sad and pathetic.

"You are angry, child."

I am no longer alone. She is suddenly beside me. Thor's maternal goddess. I don't really want to talk to anybody, but you can't tell a goddess to go away. At least, probably not without serious consequences, and I have enough of those for the moment.

"Yes, I am."

"You want revenge."

"No. Not particularly."

"Pity. I was always very good at revenge," Skathi sighs. "What are you angry at?"

Now that I know she's a goddess, I find myself biting my tongue. Doesn't seem like a good idea to annoy her. Am I afraid of her? Yes. I am not afraid of much in this world, but this woman is not of this world. She is the embodiment of deep, old, cold things, and she has an agenda.

"Your son," I say.

"Ah. He has angered you. Men often have that effect on women. And in turn, women confound men. I believe he is confounded by you."

"Is there some way of unbinding me from him? I know he doesn't want me. I took his dumb hammer because he had it out, exposed, and now because I killed someone with it..."

"No," she says.

"No?"

"The hammer is an extension of his will. Not yours. The hammer did not save you. *He* defended you. He opened up the skies to allow you to escape, and he took you into his arms. You did nothing. Except take what called to you."

"But he doesn't want me."

"Thor is a man who has never known what he wanted until he lost it. He is brave, and he is strong. He is kind, in his own way. And he is constant. But he has never known love."

"Never?"

"Never," she says. "I returned his breath to him, but there are some things that die with a person when they die. I believe the heart may be one of them. He cannot love you because he cannot love anybody."

"But he seems so normal. At least…"

"Normal. Compared to what?"

"Compared to anybody. Bryn. He's a bitter old priest…"

"I'm familiar with Father Bryn. He is not a good comparison. He is not heartless, but he is devoid of soul. Don't assume that because Thor has a better grasp of social behavior he knows how to care the way a man without his pain might."

I don't know if she is trying to make me feel better, but she is not. She is making me feel substantially worse, in fact. I can't even hope that he might come to love me, because according to this goddess, he can't.

"So what am I supposed to do?"

"You are what you are. You are where you are. And you must do what you must do."

Vague. Too vague. Useless, really. Can't tell her that, either.

Can't say anything. Can't do anything. Just have to sit and freeze in the middle of fucking nowhere. Or go back inside and try to go to sleep and hope that the dreams don't come for me again. I preferred it when I didn't have a conscience, or when I was too busy to have one.

"Anita! ANITA!"

Thor's voice roars through the night. He must have come back to the room and found me missing. Now he is shouting for me. He always wants to know where I am. I used to think that meant he liked me. Now I know it's just because he's afraid of what I'm doing.

"You should answer him," she says. "He worries, you know."

"How can he worry if he doesn't care?"

"I didn't say he didn't care. I said he didn't love. There's a difference."

"I don't want to answer him."

I don't want to be humiliated again. I don't want to mistake his possessive streak for love. I don't want to let my own feelings run amok. I just want this all to stop.

"You're certain?"

"Very."

She lifts a long finger in a direction. Could be north. Could be south. I have always been directionally challenged.

"Follow that path," she says. "You will get what you need."

Thor

I see a figure in the dark. I know it's not Anita. It's Skathi. Her silhouette is unmistakable. I run toward her, hoping she will know what is happening. There is real, cold fear inside me that Skathi may have done something to her. My mother is often ruthless with those who are not careful.

"Where is Anita?"

"I don't know," she says.

"You always know."

"Then I am not telling," she smiles.

"It is cold, and there are a thousand ways to die out here. Where is Anita?"

"You've never been able to threaten me, boy. Don't imagine you can now. If you want her, I suggest you go and claim her so she knows she has been claimed. Don't leave her wondering if you want her or not. You may think that being bound means she's a certainty, but I can assure you that is not the case. You can lose what is bound to you just as easily as you can lose something you never had at all."

That makes no sense, but she has never worried about making sense.

"She'll freeze to death out here. Please. Tell me where she went."

"You are connected, Thor. Use that connection. And as you are using it, reflect on what it means to you. And what you might do if you were never to feel it again."

"Skathi!"

Shouting her name does nothing.

"I don't know what to do with her," I sigh. "I love her, but she is such an incorrigible little shit."

"That sounds like your type, child. Now, the next time you see her, remember this feeling. Remember your love. I have told her you are not capable of it."

"Why!?"

"Because until this moment, I do not believe you were. You brought her all the way here because you could not see what was before your own nose. The hammer works for her because you work for her. She took the hammer because she knew the moment she saw it, that it belonged to her. She is yours. You are hers. You do not own her alone, Thor. You own each other. Or you did."

I look into the thick, dark night, and I know Anita is somewhere in it feeling the worst of all possible human emotions: loneliness. Not a temporary pang of feeling disconnected, but the much worse aching, deep knowledge that one belongs to nothing at all.

I have made so many mistakes. And now that it has been spelled out to me like the dullard I must be, I know I have more to atone for than I can begin to express.

"I'm going to find her," I tell Skathi. "I'm going to get her back."

Skathi says three words that bring everything into sudden sharp focus.

"It's too late."

It's not too late.

It can't be too late.

Anita

I am walking through the dark. Every step brings clarity. Thor doesn't love me. Nobody loves me. My friends abandoned me at the first sign of trouble. Bryn, who surrounds himself with demons, considers me a worthless slattern. Thor, who calls me his, does not actually want me. He wants a solution to me.

I could find that solution. I could *be* that solution. If I go away, then all of these problems go away too. Thor won't be obligated to keep me. He won't have to fly me to the ends of the earth and have his mother tell me he's not capable of love.

I am owned, maybe. But I am not wanted. And I am tired of not being wanted.

I step in something cold. Something wet. Something that makes me feel the grip of pure ice that turns oddly and nearly immediately to a perverse sense of warmth.

I'm sliding.

Slipping.

Going...

Gone.

T*hor*

I have been unspeakably stupid. I was so obsessed with the question of the hammer and why it works for Anita, I couldn't see that I loved her. That was always at the core of it. Love at first sight. It was simple. I was too stupid to know it.

I knew I lusted after her, but she was so distracting, so challenging, so obnoxious it felt as though she could not possibly truly be a part of me. Someone I loved. Someone who meant more to me than life itself.

I brought her here for clarity. Now I have clarity, but I don't have her. And it was all so obvious all along. From the moment our eyes first met and I felt not only the tingle of electric connection but the hand of fate upon me.

All she wanted was to be wanted. I see that now. I see so many yearnings and needs hidden in her horrific behavior. Every time she taunted me, she was begging for my attention, and every time she got it, she submitted perfectly. But I didn't see it. I saw a problem. I saw a pain. An obstacle.

"ANITA!" I scream her name to the night, but there is no response. She could be anywhere. I can't feel her. I can't feel anything besides regret. The longer my search goes on, the worse I feel about it. There's something permanent in the air, something irreversible. It is one of those nights on which tragedies happen.

"Thor!" It is Skathi's voice hailing me. I don't want to hear her voice now. I want to hear Anita's. For reasons I cannot put into language, hearing the goddess' voice in the night is like the tolling of a bell that cannot be unrung.

I run toward her, desperate.

"She's gone, Thor."

"NO!"

Anita is wet and blue, and blue is not a good color for people. She has been pulled from the water of the pond by my mother's hand, just as I once was. But she is not being born anew. She is lying still. She is absent.

"Did she do this on purpose?" I ask.

"The pond was covered in leaves and snow. She didn't even know she was on ice, let alone thin ice. Poor thing." There is great pity and sadness in my mother's voice.

"Save her, Skathi. Please." I am begging her, but I already know she is going to refuse. If she were to save Anita, she would have already done so. Instead, she lets the girl lie there like so much frozen meat.

Skathi looks at me. "I can't save her, Thor. Not the way I saved you. Whatever I might bring back will not be what was lost." She reaches for me with her cold hand. "I think it is time you learned what I have learned. Sometimes, it is best to let what is gone, go."

13

Anita

I'm so fucking warm. Hot, even. I'm swimming about in a thick, viscous material. Contrary to the experience of my physical form, I didn't fall into a freezing Norwegian lake. I fell into a lake of fire. But I'm not burning. I'm not suffering at all. I'm just... me. After a few minutes of generally swimming about, I hear a voice calling for me.

"Anita!"

"ANITA!"

I paddle over to the edge of the lake and climb out. Someone is waiting for me. Someone tall, dark, and handsome. I don't recognize him, or perhaps I do? He has pale skin, dark hair, and the cutest little horns poking out between his curling locks. He's obviously not human — and obviously nor am I.

"Welcome home."

"Home?"

"It's so cute when they forget," he says to nobody in particular. He smiles. "I'm Noah."

"You're a demon with a biblical name?"

"Technically, all demons have biblical names. Though you've always chosen differently, Anita."

"You know me?"

"We all know you. Like I said. You're home."

"I don't remember coming from here." I look down at myself. I am dripping lava in a very unconcerned way. I should really be melting into nothing, turning into an eternal shriek. But I'm not. I'm just here. Me.

"Nobody remembers where they come from. Now come. There are a lot of souls who have missed you in the twenty-six years since you left us. You'll start to remember as you settle in."

"There's someone I'd really like to get back to..."

The demon Noah shakes his head emphatically. "Can't do that, I'm afraid. You get one chance at a life every three hundred years. Those are the rules. You get slain or trip into a bath with a toaster, you have to wait your turn again. We can't have the whole planet becoming demon infested. It's bad for their environment."

"Oh. But what if I fell in love with someone up there?"

"We all fall in love all the time. But we know we can't hold onto that love. It's just how it is. Tell you what, torture a few unfortunates and you'll feel better, I guarantee it."

"Wait, how long did you say I have to stay down here?"

"Three hundred years."

"So ten generations. That's a lot of generations."

"Sure. If you're lucky, you can sometimes sleep with the great, great, great, great, great, great, great, great, great grandson or daughter of the one you loved before. It's a trip. Humans always underestimate how strong genetic influence is. I once had sex with a woman in ancient Egypt, and then fucked her descendant in the 1950's and they both came exactly the same way..."

He reminisces, and I do what demons do best. I start to scheme.

Thor is going to be worried sick about me. He's not going to know what happened. I don't know what happened. One moment I was wandering miserably in the woods, and the next...

Here I am, respawning in the lake of fire. The demon Noah might be right. This does feel natural. Uncomfortably comfortable, even. But I don't want to be here. I want to be with Thor. I want him to know I didn't run away and leave him. We were having a fight, and now that seems stupid. I was asking so much from him. I was demanding he have no curiosity about me and simply love me without thought. I couldn't give him one evening to come to terms with the revelations we'd come to. No. I wanted an instant happily ever after, and when I didn't get it, I went and jumped in a lake. Or rather, I fell.

"Noah?"

"Yes?"

"I can't go back to the human realm?"

"Not yet. You have to do your shifts first. A hundred years of torture, a hundred years of mockery, and a hundred years of petty bureaucracy. The latter is more painful than anything else, for you, and for the souls we are bound to punish."

"Alright, but what about goddesses. There's one up there I'd like to reckon with."

"Do not cross goddesses. Ever. We have a reputation for being unnecessarily cruel, but they take the entire proceedings to greater heights than even I can fathom."

"You mean perhaps, like telling someone to go for a walk in the woods knowing they'll fall into the same icy lake their lover's family perished in long ago?"

"Sure. That sounds like a goddess prank."

"Prank! I'm fucking dead!"

"You're not. Nobody is, technically. When it comes to the human realm, the rest of us are simply... absent. Now. Come. You look like you need a drink."

"A drink, after drowning?"

"We enjoy irony down here."

I follow him along the red rock paths carved into the underworld's geography. This place is orderly, but in a way I can't quite understand right now. There's something strange about the way the path rises and then falls and then turns about on itself and somehow I feel like I am upside down, then right side up again. It's very disorienting, but it doesn't seem to bother anybody else, so I don't let it bother me.

There is an opening carved into the wall. It is ornate, the kind of work that only happens when there's an abundance of time for overly talented people to undertake it. The human world is full of old works like this, but the newer buildings are all so ugly. Practical. Rushed. The world would be so much more beautiful if it was more like Hell.

I catch myself giggling at that thought as I am led into a raucous, rowdy tavern. Everybody is naked. I am naked too, now I think about it. I don't know why I didn't think about it before. I suppose it seemed natural.

WELCOME HOME! The message is carved into rocks hanging just inside the entrance to the subterranean bar.

"Is the sign for me?"

"Yes. But also, no. We have a constant stream of returnees. At first, we held welcome back parties, but over time they started blending into one another until it was basically one big welcome back party, so we decided to make the sign a little more permanent. It gives the humans hope for us to crush too, so that is nice."

"Nice," I agree, absent-mindedly.

The bar is full of demons, none of whom look greatly distinguishable from humans. I suppose that's why I never noticed I was one, even when people called me one to my face.

"Here. Drink." Noah shoves a massive tankard over to me.

"What is this?"

"Nectar. It's sweet, but calories don't matter here, and diabetes doesn't exist. Drink up. It will help you forget."

I had just raised the tankard to my lips. At those words, I put it back down again. I don't want to forget. And I don't want to be here, as comfortable as here already feels. I want to be back with Thor.

Noah drains his cup, then grabs my tankard and drinks it deep. "I'll get you another," he says. He does. And then he drinks that too. And then he starts to dance with the others and then I am forgotten.

I sit at the bar and I think. I want out of here. I belong here, but I don't want to be here. Is that what love is? Does it make the familiar feel wrong? Does it inspire one to be better? That last part sounds right.

I tortured Thor the entire time I knew him. I made his life hell. And his mother disposed of me. She must have seen right through me. I'm not angry at her. I think I might have done the same were I her. I'm not good for him. He's probably better and happier without me.

"Another?"

The demon behind the counter is a stunning blonde man. I am surrounded by gorgeous men and women, and an atmosphere of support and acceptance. I don't make anybody here angry. I can't. We're all the same.

"Please."

Another tankard comes across the counter. This time I pick it up, and I drink.

14

Thor

"It is for the best, my child. She was not made for you, and you were not made for her."

How could this outcome be for the best? And at the same time, how could this have ended any other way? I knew the moment I first laid eyes on her that she was trouble. I watched her behave recklessly, barely surviving scrape after scrape. Until this one. The one she could not survive.

I carried her back from the lake, cold and stiff. Now she is wrapped in linens, stored away neatly. One of my things.

I told her that, once. More than once. I made it very apparent she was a belonging of mine. Not a person to be loved. A thing to be had. And used. And in the end, she chose the darkness of the night. If it was a choice at all. Maybe it was just an inevitability, a cruel reminder from the universe itself that I did not deserve the heat of her passion, or the intensity of her existence.

Grief has become my only temperament and mood. It has crawled into every orifice, sunk into every pore. I am pickled in it. I stink of it. And I cannot escape it.

"I need to return to Direford. It is where she came from. It is where she should be returned."

Skathi inclines her head in agreement. "That may be best, my son. The embrace of the Brotherhood and the work of your brothers will heal what the world has taken from you. It is best you focus on your calling, Thor. This was an unfortunate interlude, but as I understand it, a short one."

"A week, I think. Beginning to end. Sunday to Sunday."

"Sometimes the shortest things in life affect us the deepest," she acknowledges.

"Sometimes things are gone before you know what they were."

"Don't imagine that you loved her more than you did simply because she's dead. That's a very human mistake to make. Let yourself grieve and move on. If you want to take a bride at some point, you can find someone more suited. Someone less chaotic. Someone with elegance and breeding."

She's trying to distract me with visions of a future we both know I'll never have. I'm not made for nice women with good temperaments and whatever she means by breeding. I was made for that rough and ready streak of pure feminine madness who could not be contained, who took me by the shaft and turned my world upside down. I wonder what would have happened if I'd just let her hold my hammer in the first place. If I hadn't tried to fight what was between us.

She might still be here. That moment was explosive in so many ways, and I didn't see it for what it was.

~

A *flight later...*
"Welcome home, brother."

Bryn embraces me, but I don't feel his hug. I don't feel anything anymore. There's a numbness where feelings used to be.

"I'm sorry," he says. "I know you were fond of her."

Words are always too little in these situations. Bryn's words somehow manage to be less than too little. I don't blame him. There's nothing he could say now that would make a difference.

Crichton and Crocombe appear to be hearing this information for the first time. Crocombe lets out a sigh and buries her face in Crichton's chest. The two of them have never gotten along, but grief bonds in a way happiness cannot. He murmurs something in her ear, something that makes her look up quickly and nod. Then he disappears.

I'd worry, but I'm not capable of worrying anymore. I have lost my ability to care. I may not ever care again. I might not be capable of it. I might be internally cold and frozen forever.

15

Anita

I don't know how much nectar I have had. Not enough, because I can still remember Thor very clearly. Noah promised me I'd forget, but I don't think I can. Whatever is supposed to be working down here is not working. I'm not surprised. That's how most things in the world are when it comes to me. My contrariness extends to the underworld, so it seems.

I'm starting to ask myself questions. Questions like, what's stopping me from leaving, exactly? I don't know the official way out, but I do know that there's probably a lot of them. Crichton just snapped one open when he needed it, and nobody seemed to have any issue with that. I'm wondering if the three hundred years thing is more like a guideline than a hard and fast enforced rule.

Time is hard to keep track of here, and I'm frankly not certain how long I have been drinking. There is music, a steady drumbeat that might represent time. I'm yet to make any friends, though Noah said many here knew me. Hell is a surprisingly lonely place.

I go for a walk. The burning lava lakes are nice this time of year, so people keep saying to one another. I find myself indifferent to the suffering of the souls in the lakes and various locations. I suppose I should be horrified. If I were a good person, I would be. But I'm not a person. I never have been — and that explains a lot.

I find myself looking up, my gaze drawn to the surface world I am not permitted to inhabit. The nectar may have taken the edge off my memory, but it has done nothing to stop the yearning grief that lives at my core.

What's stopping me from leaving, exactly? I don't know. Escape must be possible. I try to think of ways I've seen escapes take place from prisons. Usually there's some digging involved. I can dig. I can dig straight up. It's a simple, mechanistic solution to the problem, but it might just work.

I start to dig a passage up through the red rock. I do it with my bare hards, clawing at the rock and shoving it to the side. It's surprising how much progress I make in a relatively short period of time.

"There's no point."

"What?" I turn my head to look at Noah, who has returned to conveniently spread his message of despair. I wonder if he's watching me. Keeping an eye on me.

"You could dig for a thousand years and never reach the surface. The only way to escape, if that's what you're trying to do, is to have someone let you out from over there."

"So someone has to come for me? Has to want me back on Earth?"

"Exactly. Demons are summoned. If someone up there wants you, you'll be back before you know it. If you've been forgotten, you'll be here for three hundred years."

"But someone would have to know I'm a demon — and I didn't even know that. So..."

"Yes. Very difficult. Anyway..." He wanders off, leaving me with aching fingers and a great deal of red dust in every orifice.

Will someone summon me? Thor won't. He doesn't know to. Bryn won't. He doesn't want me back. Anita won't. I have so few allies in the world, no friends, and maybe...

Wait. There's something in my hole. Something is coming wriggling through it. Several somethings. Wriggling things, making their way through the rock and soil. I recoil and think about hitting the wriggling things, but they swiftly become fingers, and then a hand.

I can't see a face. I can't see anything more than an understated brown suit and a perfectly pressed cuff, but I know who it is immediately. I grab that hand. I am dragged up through the soil of Hell, my being dragged from one world to another. It hurts. It hurts like nothing I have ever felt before. Everything in me tells me to let go, that the pain will stop if I just resign myself to my fate.

But there's no way I am doing that. This pain is the price that has to be paid for getting free. I cling to the hand. I hold onto it for dear life. And suddenly, as if the universe has finally accepted that my will is stronger than death, the pain ends and I emerge through a familiar floor, into a cell I once occupied a literal lifetime ago.

Crichton still has my hand. I can't let go. My fingers are cramped around his in a death grip. He doesn't seem to mind.

"It is good to see you again, miss," he says in that understated English way of his.

"Fuck that," I say, leaping on him. I hold onto him just as hard as I held onto Thor. Maybe harder. This demon has been nothing short of my salvation. "Thank you so much. I owe you more than I can say, I..."

"Yes, very gratifying," Crichton says, as if the whole thing is a bit embarrassing to him. "I'm afraid you will have to get cleaned up and dressed rather quickly. You're late."

"What can I possibly be late for?"

16

hor

"Ashes to ashes... dust to dust."

I brought Anita back to Direford to be laid to rest. It was her home, and it should be where she spends eternity. The journey was a silent and cold one. I wished more than anything that she was there to say something impertinent and improper, to show me a lack of respect. I'd let her do whatever she liked just to see her do something, anything, ever again.

But that time is over. I squandered it. I took her to a place of cold death and cold death claimed her. It is my fault. It has been my fault from the very beginning.

Somewhere in the background, the old man is droning the rites. A pine box contains what is left of my loved one. It is all so mundane. So simple. So mechanical. Sometimes people seem to be larger than life, creatures of light and meaning. But at times like this, they are like wound-down toys with broken springs. There is no putting them back together, no matter how much you love them.

"We are gathered here today to say farewell to Anita... Lastnameunknown."

Steven pronounces it as if it is all one word. How does he not know her name? Why has her loss left so little a ripple in the world? I would prefer Bryn had taken the funeral, but the fog has returned with the turning of the seasons, and as usual, Bryn has become paranoid and insists that he needs to be armed in case of attack. He is correct that demonic activity increases around this time, but surely the chapel at Direview Abbey is not one of the places demons are likely to attack.

With mist swirling about my ankles like waifs from other realms tugging at my legs to get my attention, I do not have the energy to fight him. I do not have the energy to do anything besides stand here and watch as the love of my life is lowered into the ground, my one chance at true happiness being sent back to the earth from which she came.

"What are we doing?" Someone whispers the question in my ear. Someone who sounds more than a little confused.

"It's a funeral."

"Oh. Who died?"

I turn around. Anita is standing before me, curls shining in the sun.

"... You."

"Well, this is awkward," she grins.

She's in the fucking coffin. I know she's in the coffin. But she's also standing in front of me. I grab her and pull her close, feeling the impossible flesh of her body against mine. She's alive. She's here. I draw in her scent. She smells the same. It is as though everything in Norway never happened, as if some cosmic reset button as been pressed. I am so happy tears are running down my face. I don't recall crying ever in my life. I did not think it was possible. I thought it was part of the curse and the gift and the coldness.

"DEMON!"

Bryn comes flying through the air like a vengeful madman, sword drawn. He's managed to lose his shirt, and the swirling fog flails and curls in the wake of his mad rush.

Having had Anita return to me against all odds, I am not going to stand by and watch her be sent back to Hell. Returning from that realm is no easy feat. I swing her around behind me and put myself between her and Bryn's sword. My hand is on the shaft of my hammer and it, too, is raised aloft, ready to command the winds and the rains, the thunder and the lightning. I will bring the world itself down on his head to protect her if I have to.

My hammer comes to me, splintering out of the coffin where I laid it to rest with her body. I had decided to give myself up, and give her what she wanted so badly, what she was prepared to die for. It has killed for her before, and it will kill for her again.

Bryn stops, seething with his fog rage. In times like these, he his not himself. He is a tool of the divine, and he is more impossible to argue with than ever. I will kill him if I have to, and I will experience no remorse for having done so.

"She's a demon." He snarls the words, practically salivating with the desire to end her.

"I don't care what she is. She's mine, and I love her."

"Bryn!" Nina intervenes. "You can't slay the loves of people's lives. This is a funeral. Show some decorum."

She joins me, standing between me and him, her red-headed beauty perhaps the only thing capable of stilling Bryn's blade. He and I are both made weaker and better by our love.

Anita's arms are wrapped around me. She does not want to let go any more than I do. She looks up into my face, ignoring Bryn as the irrelevance he is.

"Just so you know, I'm not supposed to be here. I've skipped the queue. They're going to be looking for me."

"Well, they'd be stupid to try to get you at Direview. We're demon hunters, and occasionally, we do slay a demon."

"She's a demon!" Bryn shouts.

"Yes, and so is Crichton, and Crocombe. Think about it. At least you know how to control demons. You have no idea how to handle people. This is actually a positive step," Nina says.

I'm only barely listening to anything going on around us. All I can think of is how desperately fortunate I am to have her back with me.

"I am never going to let you go. And I am never, ever going to let you think you are anything other than wanted and adored, do you understand me, Anita?"

"Why do you still sound like you're lecturing me, even when you're happy?"

"I don't know. It's just the way I've become accustomed to talking to you."

"So are we still burying the body, or...." Steven asks the question, but it is lost to the wind.

I sweep Anita up off her feet and I carry her away, back to Direview, back to the place we will both call home.

17

Thor

"Are you sure you want me?"

The question hurts to hear, but I cannot pretend to be surprised she asks it. It was my apparent indifference that led her to the lake. I lectured her over and over about being safe and sane and sensible and in the end I acted like an emotional mute.

"I want you," I tell her, holding her hands and looking deep into her eyes, where mischief still perpetually dances. "I always wanted you. I let too many things get in the way. I was confused. I was stupid. I was distracted by the death in the village... I let what I thought was right stand between what was right in front of me. I've never been able to resist you, Anita, and I am more sorry than I can say that I couldn't express that before you..."

"Yes," she says with a wicked little grin. "Let's call it my journey of self-discovery, shall we?"

Euphemisms for death, separation, and suffering make them all easier to bear.

"Can you really be with me, now that you know what I am? Your kind is sworn to slay me. I don't think I am going to get any easier to be around. I think I'm going to probably be worse. I'm a demon. And now I know that absolutely everything makes sense. Thor, it's so liberating!"

"The only part of you I'll be slaying is..."

"Oh no!" She laughs. "Don't say that. It's so crude. You're better than that, Thor Larsen."

I'm not better than that. I am not better than her. I crave her, and I have to be inside her.

"I should never have stopped making love to you," I growl. "Every time I was inside you, everything was right. And every time we stopped I was distracted by all the things I thought I knew..."

She's stripping her clothes off. She pauses as I pause, her sweater half off over her head, one eye exposed. "I'm sorry," she says. "Did you want to keep talking, or..."

I do not want to keep talking.

∾

"Mine," I growl, sinking inside the hot, wet chalice of her sex. Yes, I am fucking a demon. Yes, she is writhing beneath me, spreading her legs and arching herself up to me, making incoherent sounds of needy delight. Yes, I have her pinned beneath me so she cannot go anywhere, so her submission must be as complete as my possession.

Her eyes are alight with pure desire. Her legs wrap themselves around my waist as she draws herself up to me, clinging to me with all four limbs. There is still a desperation between us. It is not enough for us to have been reunited. We are terrified that we will lose one another, that at any moment fate might intervene and snatch her away.

Life does not often give second chances of this kind. I drive deep inside her, stretching her wide, feeling her grip me with that molten inner strength that makes it almost impossible for me to hold back from spending myself inside her.

"I love you," I say for what must be the hundredth time since I carried her off.

"I love you too," she whimpers. She's so close. I can see heat suffusing her face, turning her pale skin pink. I want to hear her say that for the rest of my life and whatever might come beyond it.

"Don't let go," I tell her, pulling my cock out to the very entrance of her pussy. I need a break, and she needs to remember that I am in control.

"Please..." she whimpers desperately. "Don't make me wait. I don't know that I have time to wait. We have to take what we can here, now, while we have a here and a now."

I pull my cock free of her tight cunt and deprive us both of what we crave. I have some kind of sadistic streak that clearly now transcends sadism and is traversing the wild territory of masochism. I will torture myself in order to torture her. This thing between us has enough power to transcend death. We can hold off a few seconds. I look down at her with deep satisfaction and even more desire. Every instant my throbbing cock remains outside her is one in which I feel myself torn with need. She is in the same state. She spreads her legs wider and tries to wriggle herself onto my rod, but I don't allow that. I want her to know that I am still master of her desires, and mine. I want the dynamic we had before, the one that had just begun to nourish us both, to be reestablished.

"Please, Thor. Let me have it. Let me have you."

She asked so nicely. So prettily. How can I refuse? I snatch her wrists up above her head and look down at her sweat slaked body. A fresh form given to her in the depths of Hades now arches for me, generous breasts and the soft swell of hip and thigh framing her wet cunt. I need her like I need air.

"FUCK!"

She curses as I drive inside her, splitting her open, giving her my cock, and taking pleasure from her tightness. I pound into her, letting my lust and my need and my joy and my sadness and the stubborn lingering shreds of guilt and grief melt away in the inferno of our mutual orgasm.

A*nita*

We are steaming gently in the aftermath of our love. The room is cold due to the windows all being wide open, and we are warm. Our breath curls and coils into the atmosphere.

"Tell me again how it happened," Thor prompts me.

"I fell into a lake of fire, and eventually, it felt like a lot longer than it was, Crichton came for me. I don't think I would ever have freed myself on my own. They said I owed them three hundred years. I don't know that they'll actually notice me missing, but if they do keep track, I am probably in trouble."

"I don't think there is any doubt you would be in trouble. Being in trouble is your natural state."

"True," I agree.

There is a light tap at the door.

"Come in!" Thor calls out. I cuddle naked next to him, wondering who has the nerve to interrupt our copulatory marathon.

"If the two of you have enjoyed your carnal reunion, Father Bryn requests the pleasure of your presence," Crichton says. "Actually, he wishes to speak to Anita alone, but I doubted you would allow that, sir. Given what happened at the funeral."

"Given he tried to kill me at my own funeral, which I think we can all agree is just gauche."

"Indeed."

"I doubt he wants to make an apology, but we do need to come to some kind of terms with each other," Thor says. "We should go and talk to him. The fog has receded. He will be something closer to sane by now."

∼

Bryn and Nina are in the dining room. It looks as though they have been enjoying a mutual dessert in the middle of the day. Bryn is sitting at the head of the table, with Nina to his right. She gives me a big smile. I smile back at her, but not Bryn. I'm really not sure how this complete plonker makes her happy, but he does seem to.

"There is only one kind of demon tolerated in this house," Bryn says, launching into his little speech without so much as a greeting. Does it not occur to him that he is unspeakably rude? Here I am back from the dead and I can't get so much as a *happy you're alive.* He's never liked me, but he doesn't need to make it so obvious. "And that is a service demon. If you want to dwell here, Anita, you must learn to serve. Is that understood? And is it agreeable?"

It is not agreeable.

"What would you do if it wasn't? Slay me? Send me back to Hell? You know everybody in this household wants me here. Thor would literally kill you if you tried to hurt me. I don't have to serve anyone. If you want to call me a service demon to make yourself feel better, knock yourself out. But I'd be back here in a matter of days even if you did slay me."

Bryn looks at Thor as if expecting some kind of backup, but Thor is still absolutely drenched in guilt from letting me die in the Nordic dark, and he is not going to tell me to mind Bryn.

"I think it is just so romantic that you came all the way back from Hell for Thor," Nina sighs. "You are truly meant for one another. Death itself cannot separate you. I love Bryn just as much, but there's no demonstration like that. You have proof of one of the great loves."

She really is a soft and sappy little thing underneath it all.

"She's a demon," Bryn reminds her. "She didn't survive death. She was made of it."

"Listen, that's not my fault. I didn't get any choice in my existence, no more than you did, or a frog does. I am me, and you're the only one who seems to have a problem with it."

"The Brotherhood has splintered over my lax attitude to demons. This is a step further than any of them would ever tolerate. It is one thing to have servant demons working their way toward mortality through service, but a recalcitrant little wench with no interest in the welfare of th..."

"I didn't say I had no interest in your stupid welfare."

"Very diplomatic," Thor murmurs in my ear.

"Besides, for demon hunters, you're very bad at knowing when you're in the presence of a demon. So it's not as if any of them will know. You might be the worst collection of demon hunters that ever demon hunted, to be frank."

Bryn's expression grows ever more thunderous, until Nina reaches over and puts her hand gently on his arm.

"We don't always like what love looks like," she says. "But we know when we are in its presence, and this is love."

She's like a walking greeting card, but I'm not going to point that out in my typically cynical fashion. She's on our side, and I am certain that she is the only person capable of containing Bryn. Left to his own devices, he would be one of the most destructive forces on the planet. She moderates him.

I wonder if Thor will moderate me. Will I become pleasingly domestic? Another of Direview's captive brides gleefully living my life at the carnal pleasure of my master? The idea doesn't sound entirely terrible. It might even be something akin to a happily ever after.

"Are you going to say anything about this?" I nudge an elbow gently back against his midsection.

"I have no words to describe what I would do for you," Thor says. "The Brotherhood is not my concern anymore. I do not care about the petty infighting of men who should know better, who should forgive more, who should understand that our primary role is to do good in this world, and the next."

Bryn sighs. "So this is how it is to be? A demon hunting brotherhood outnumbered by demons in their own home?"

"It would appear so, brother," Thor says without a hint of regret.

"May as well declare ourselves a demon rescue, a rehabilitation service for doomed souls," Bryn sighs, even deeper than before. He is coming to terms with things being as they are, the infinite inevitability of me.

"Right, then, Thor and I are going back to bed," I declare, sliding my hand into Thor's great paw. "If you need anything, don't call us."

"My little demon." Thor purrs against my neck.

We are barely back in the privacy of his bed chamber before he is buried inside me, my hot core wrapped around his rock-hard rod. I will spend an eternity like this, fucking him, being fucked by him and being loved forever.

"Thor..."

"Yes?" He grunts in my ear, his hips stilling.

"Can I still be wanted for murder if I'm dead?"

"Don't worry about the law," he growls, pinning me down and plunging his cock slowly in and out of me. "I am your law now. I am your beginning, and your end. I will summon you, and you will come. Do you understand me?"

He starts hammering inside me, driving me toward a vicious orgasm that will not be denied. I feel the hot, hard heat of his cock pounding inside me, my demonic flesh all too human for this perfect coupling.

"Come for me. Now. COME!" His orders ring in my ears like thunder.

I have no choice but to obey. I come hard, clenching him deep inside my body, draining him of his seed, joining him as an equal partner in all things eternal.

Made in the USA
Coppell, TX
18 October 2022